A TREASURY OF
SPOOKY
STORIES

Kingfisher Books, Grisewood & Dempsey Ltd,
Elsley House, 24–30 Great Titchfield Street,
London W1P 7AD

First published in 1992 by Kingfisher Books
4 6 8 10 9 7 5

BRITISH LIBRARY CATALOGUING IN PUBLICATION DATA
A catalogue record for this book is available from the British Library

ISBN 0 86272 973 4

Phototypeset by Southern Postives and Negatives
(SPAN), Lingfield, Surrey
Printed and bound in Spain

A TREASURY OF
SPOOKY
STORIES

Chosen by
JANE OLLIVER

Illustrated by
ANNABEL SPENCELEY

Kingfisher Books

CONTENTS

THE GUITARIST

Grace Hallworth

Joe was always in demand for the Singings, or community evenings held in villages which were too far away from the city to enjoy its attractions. He was an excellent guitarist and when he wasn't performing on his own, he accompanied the singers and dancers who also attended the Singing.

After a Singing someone was sure to offer Joe a lift back to his village but on one occasion he found himself stranded miles away from his home with no choice but to set out on foot. It was a dark night and there wasn't a soul to be seen on the road, not even a cat or a dog, so Joe began to strum his guitar to hearten himself for the lonely journey ahead.

Joe had heard many stories about strange things seen at night on that road but he told himself that most of the people who related these stories had been drinking heavily. All the same, as he came to a crossroad known to be the haunt of Lajables and other restless spirits, he strummed his guitar loudly to drown the rising clamour of fearful thoughts in his head. In the quiet of early morning the tune was sharp and strong, and Joe began to move to the rhythm; but all the while his eyes were fixed on a point ahead of him where four roads met. The nearer he got, the more convinced he was that someone was standing in the middle of the road. He hoped with all his heart that he was wrong and that the shape was only a shadow cast by an overhanging tree.

The man stood so still he might have been a statue, and it was only when Joe was within arm's length of the figure that he saw any sign of life. The man was quite tall, and so thin that his clothes hung on him as though they were thrown over a wire frame. There was a musty smell about them. It was too dark to see who the man was or what he looked like, and when he spoke his voice had a rasp to it which set Joe's teeth on edge.

"You play a real fine guitar for a youngster," said the man, falling into step beside Joe.

Just a little while before, Joe would have given anything to meet another human being but somehow he was not keen to have this man as a companion. Nevertheless his motto was "Better to be safe than sorry," so he was as polite as his unease would allow.

"It's nothing special but I like to keep my hand in. What about you, man? Can you play guitar too?" asked Joe.

"Let me try your guitar and we'll see if I can match you," replied the man.

Joe handed over his guitar and the man began to play so gently and softly that Joe had to listen closely to hear the tune. He had never heard such a mournful air. But soon the music changed, the tune became wild and the rhythm fast and there was a harshness about it which drew a response from every nerve in Joe's body. Suddenly there was a new tone and mood and the music became light and enchanting. Joe felt as if he were borne in the air like a blown-up balloon. He was floating on a current of music and would follow it to the ends of the earth and beyond.

And then the music stopped. Joe came down to earth with a shock as he realised that he was standing in front of his house. The night clouds were slowly dispersing. The man handed the guitar back to Joe who was still dazed.

"Man, that was guitar music like I never heard in this world before," said Joe.

"True?" said the man. "You should have heard me when I was alive!"

IN A DARK, DARK BOX

Jane Hollowood

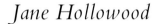

Once upon a time there was an old grandmother, who lived quite alone in a little dark house in the middle of a wood. One day her grandson came to stay.

The boy had never visited his grandmother before. When he arrived, late one evening, he felt very strange and very shy, and of course very tired, too, after his long journey. As it was so late, Grandmother took him straight upstairs – up the winding staircase and along a dark, creaky passage to his bedroom.

"Here we are," she said, throwing open the door. "Now you get undressed and into bed and I'll bring you up some supper." And she shuffled off downstairs.

The boy got into his pyjamas and climbed into the narrow wooden bed. He looked around the room, but it was lit only by a candle, and the corners were so black and shadowy that he could scarcely make out what was what. Outside, the wind howled around the house and the rain drummed against the window panes. He began to feel lonely and even a bit scared. He was glad when at last Grandmother came back with his supper. She set the tray on his knee, sat down by the bed, and took up her knitting.

"Lovely pig's trotter soup and a piece of caraway seed cake," she said. "Eat them up, and I'll stay and keep you company."

She began to knit, and as she did so, she stared and stared at him over her knitting, so that the boy felt more uncomfortable than ever. He tried to sip his soup, but it tasted bitter and stuck in his throat. He glanced around the room, wishing that he could think of something to say – anything to break the silence.

Suddenly Grandmother spoke. "Shall I tell you a story?" she asked. Before he could answer, she began.

"Once upon a time there was a dark, dark wood ..."

She stopped and smiled. "Ah," she sighed. "This is like old times. I used to tell *him* stories too, every night, in this very room." She held up the candle to a picture on the wall, a photograph of a fine young man in a sailor's uniform. "That's your father," she explained. "The last photograph ever taken of him. And this was his bedroom when he was a little boy like you."

The boy wanted to jump out of bed and look at the picture more closely. His father had been drowned at sea while he was still a baby, and he had always longed to know what he had looked like. But Grandmother was starting to tell the story again, in her strange sing-song voice.

"Once upon a time there was a dark, dark wood," she began again, and at once there was a tap-tapping noise on the window. The boy jumped nervously.

"What was that?"

"Just a branch tapping on the window," said Grandmother. She started the story *again*.

"Once upon a time there was a dark, dark Wood,"

(Again, the branch tapped on the window.)

"And in the dark, dark Wood was a dark, dark House,

And in the dark, dark House was a dark, dark Hall,

And in the dark, dark Hall were some dark, dark Stairs."

(As she spoke these words, the stairs seemed to creak.)

"And up the dark, dark Stairs was a dark, dark Passage."

(At this, there was a loud crack-crack from the passage outside the bedroom door. The boy looked anxiously at Grandmother, but she hadn't noticed.)

"And in the dark, dark Passage was a dark, dark Door."

(The boy looked at the door. Did the handle turn, or was it his imagination?)

"And through the dark, dark Door, was a dark, dark ROOM!"

At the word 'room' there came a gust of wind, which sent the curtains billowing, the branch tapping, the candle flame flickering. The boy dropped his soup spoon with fright.

"I'm sorry," he said, as Grandmother picked it up for him. "The wind startled me, that's all."

Grandmother nodded and smiled, and continued with the story.

"And in the dark, dark Room was a dark, dark Cupboard."

(The boy peered into one of the black, shadowy corners, and there *was* a cupboard. He couldn't help thinking that the poem seemed to be about this very house. Everything fitted.)

"And in the dark, dark Cupboard, was a dark, dark Trunk."

That was it. He would go and see if there *was* a trunk in the cupboard. He started to get out of bed, "Let me see!" he said, but Grandmother held him back.

"Don't be silly!" she said. "How could my story be about this house, eh? It's just a silly poem that everybody knows. I expect the boys and girls at your school know it, don't they?"

The boy nodded.

"So how could it possibly be about here?"

"It's just that everything in the poem is in this house," said the boy.

Grandmother laughed. "Well, I don't see what's so odd about that," she said. "All houses have doors and stairs and passages."

"Yes, but they don't all have a trunk in the

cupboard, do they?" replied the boy. "That really would be a coincidence." And once again he tried to get out of bed to look in the cupboard, and once again Grandmother held him back.

"But there is a trunk in the cupboard," she said, laughing again. "Your father's old toy trunk."

The boy stared at her, too surprised to speak.

"Come along, lie down!" she said. "You're tired out. I'll finish the story quickly, and then you must go to sleep."

So she continued.

"And in the dark, dark Cupboard was a dark, dark Trunk,

And in the dark, dark Trunk was a dark, dark
BOX."

At this, there was a really tremendous gust of
wind, which blew the window right open and sent
the tapping branch thrusting right into the room,
like the fingers of a hand. The boy screamed out
loud, and buried his head under the bedclothes, and
Grandmother hurried across to shut the window.

"Dratted wind!" she muttered. "Whenever it
blows from the north it blows the window open and
lets in the branch and the rain." She turned back to
the room, and her face was streaming with rain
water. She walked swiftly to the door.

"Well now. That really is enough excitement for one day. No more silly stories." She went out into the passage.

The boy jumped out of bed and ran after her. "Wait!" he called. "You still haven't finished the story. What was in the box?"

"Aha!" said Grandmother, mysteriously, as she started down the stairs.

"Is there really a box inside the trunk?" the boy shouted after her. "At least tell me that."

Grandmother turned back half-way down the stairs, and looked at him in the darkness. "Do you mean, 'Is there a Box in the Trunk in the story?' or do you mean, 'Is there a real box in the real trunk?,'" she laughed to herself, and went on down the stairs, leaving the boy standing in the dark passage, all alone.

He groped his way back to his bedroom. The shadows seemed even blacker than before, the wind fairly roared against the window, the branch tap-tapped, and the rain drummed against the panes.

He stood beside the bed trying to think sensibly. "I'm just being silly," he told himself. "Granny's right. Of course the poem isn't about here. *Here* is real life, and in real life you can't be inside a poem, can you?" And he decided to look in the trunk, for once and for all, to prove to himself that there wasn't a box in it. The Box in the Trunk was in the poem, wasn't it?

He lifted the trunk and set it carefully on the floor. He stared at the lid, not quite daring to open it.

Suddenly a deep voice spoke. "Go on. Don't be frightened," it said. "Open it!"

The boy froze to the spot. He forced himself to

look around the room to see where the voice had come from, but he could see no one. "I'm imagining things," he told himself. "It must have been the wind." And he opened the lid of the trunk.

Inside he saw the strangest assortment of old-fashioned toys – a battered rag doll with one eye missing, a wind-up train, a money box, a Mr. Punch puppet – and on top of them all, looking much newer than anything else in the trunk, a box. It was quite a large box, done up with tissue paper and string, like a present which had never been opened. The boy gasped. First there had been the cupboard, then the trunk, then the box.

"Everything fits," he whispered. "There is a Box. I *am* in a poem." And he seemed to hear Grand-

mother, far, far off, laughing.

He tore off the string and the tissue paper, and underneath he found a second box, a pretty wooden box with boats painted on it and a little metal fastening. And as he looked at it, he heard the same deep voice as before, only this time it was much closer, and definitely could not be mistaken for the wind.

"Please," it said. "Please open the box and look inside."

Again the boy forced himself to look around the room. When he looked up at the photograph of his father on the wall, he saw, to his terror, that the picture had changed. Oh, how horrible it looked! Father's face and hair streamed with water, as if he were drowning, and his mouth gasped for air, and his eyes bulged, and his hands clawed and clutched, as if they were trying to fight their way through seaweed and wreckage to the surface of the sea. A trickle of water ran down the wall from the picture, and across the floor toward the trunk.

The boy cowered on the floor and hid his face, too terrified to move. All the time the voice begged him and begged him to open the box, so piteously that at last the boy could bear it no longer and took up the box and opened it.

And at once there was a great clap of wind, and the room was plunged into darkness. The curtains billowed, the door banged; the cupbord opened and shut and opened and shut. Then just as suddenly the commotion died down, and the candle flame flickered up again. The boy found himself holding a little painted wooden sailor doll. It had bright twinkly eyes and a big smile.

The deep voice spoke again. "Take it. It's yours. I made it for you. I've been waiting to give it to you, waiting for you to come, for years and years."

The boy looked up and saw his father standing in front of him, as if he had stepped down out of the picture. His splendid uniform was covered with pieces of seaweed, and dripped with water, making a puddle on the floor. He held out his arms to the boy, as if he wanted to hold him and hug him.

The boy dropped the sailor doll and tried to scream for help, but no sound would come out of his mouth. He tried to run to the door, but his legs seemed heavy as lead and he tripped over the trunk, spilling the toys across the floor. He struggled on all fours, with his father's voice in his ear, entreating him to stay, begging him to pick up the little sailor doll.

At last he reached the door, but a wrinkled hand held the door knob fast and he could not get out. He tore at the hand until at last he succeeded in pulling it away, and hurled himself out of the room. The door swung shut behind him. The voices stopped. He stood in the dark passage, listening to the silence and the pounding of his own heart.

After a bit he tip-toed to the top of the stairs, and peered down. There was Grandmother, sitting in the kitchen, rocking to and fro in her rocking chair.

He called out to her loudly, begging her to come upstairs and rescue him, but she carried on knitting without even looking up, as if she could not hear him. And from far, far off, her voice floated through the air, laughing and laughing.

He was too frightened to go down to her. Was she a witch? He stood in the darkness, uncertain what to do.

Suddenly his bedroom door opened of its own accord, and a beam of bright light fell across the passage. He heard a new voice, talking crossly to itself.

"Who on earth's been meddling with my trunk," it was saying. "They've emptied all my toys out, and they haven't even bothered to clear up!"

The boy stole to the doorway and looked at his bedroom. What a transformation! A cosy fire burned in the grate. Lamps shone in each corner. Someone else's clothes hung over the chair. In the middle of the room sat a boy in sailor clothes, a boy of about his own age, only ... only ... the boy didn't look quite real. He looked – well, almost transparent. A ghost-boy! And all the while he was busily putting the toys back in the trunk and grumbling to himself. "How dare people trespass!" he said. "This is *my* bedroom. These are *my* things."

Then the boy at the door understood. This was his father too. His father had slept in this bedroom when he was a boy. Just then the father-ghost-boy came across the little wooden sailor doll lying on the floor, and picked it up in great surprise. "Ha ha!" he said. "Whoever it was who played with my toys has left one of their own behind." And he laughed. "Well, I shall keep it! Serves them right! I'll write them a message instead and put it in the box for them to find if they ever come back."

So the ghost-boy stood the little wooden sailor doll on the window sill to keep for himself, and then he wrote a message on a scrap of paper and popped it into the pretty painted box, and he shut up the box and tossed it into the trunk. At once everything in the room crackled and shook and creaked and groaned, and the ghost-boy vanished quite away. The cosy fire vanished too, and the lamps, and the ghost-boy's clothes over the chair. The trunk jumped back into the cupboard, and Grandmother's voice floated in from far, far away, saying:

"The dark, dark Box is in the dark, dark Trunk,
    The dark, dark Trunk is in the dark, dark Cupboard,

The dark, dark Cupboard is in the dark, dark Corner,

The dark, dark Corner is in the dark, dark Room."

The boy felt himself being dragged along backward through the poem, along the dark, dark passage, down the dark, dark stairs, across the dark, dark hall. Grandmother's voice continued in its strange sing-song fashion:

"And the dark, dark Hall is in the dark, dark House,

And the dark, dark House is in the dark, dark Wood!"

Grandmother's voice rose to a shriek on these words, and the boy found himself flat on his back under the trees in the wood, and rain poured down onto his face.

Then it was morning.

There was Grandmother, drawing back the curtains and letting the sunlight flood into the room. The birds sang; the sky was blue; the world was washed clean and bright.

"Well I never!" exclaimed Grandmother, looking at the boy. "Whatever are you doing on the floor?"

The boy sat up sleepily, and sure enough, found himself in a tumble of bedclothes at the foot of his bed, as if he had fallen out in his sleep. He was just going to snuggle back down again when sudddenly he was wide awake. The night! The strange happenings! He looked quickly around the room for the trunk.

"Oh! You've put it away," he said. "And all the toys."

Grandmother laughed. "We never had any toys out," she said. "What nonsense you talk. Come along. Get dressed and you can come down for your breakfast. Toys indeed! Sleeping on the floor indeed!" And she chuckled to herself as she began to tidy up the bed.

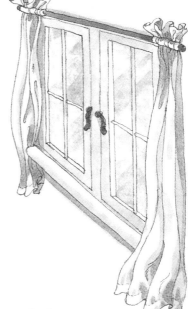

The boy rubbed his eyes, feeling very puzzled. *Was* he talking nonsense? He looked around the room again, and under the picture he saw – a puddle of water. "There! Look!" he cried. "There's the water, where he stood."

"Where who stood?"

"Father. Dripping wet and drowning!" And the boy told Grandmother all about his night, and about how he had seen his father, first as a man, and then as a boy in a sailor suit, and about the little wooden sailor doll in the box (like the Box in the poem) that Father had made for him.

Grandmother stared at him, and her eyes grew round with astonishment. Then she put her arm around him and sat him down next to her on the bed.

"Hush, child, hush," she said. "This is all in your imagination."

"It isn't. It isn't," cried the boy. "It really happened. Look, I can prove it. There *is* the little sailor doll." And he pointed over to the window sill where the ghost-boy had put it. But the window sill was empty. The little sailor doll had gone. "But ... it was there, I'm sure," he faltered, feeling more and more confused. "At least ... well, it must have been a ghost toy ... and my father ... and the boy in the sailor suit ... they were ghosts too ..."

At this Grandmother really did laugh, a big hearty laugh. "There are no such things as ghosts! You know that," she said. "You've been dreaming. That's what you've been doing. Just dreaming."

She explained how he had been tired last night, and how everything had been strange and new, and how the wind and rain battered about the window,

and how on top of all that she had told him the silly story. "So you see," she said, "it's not surprising that you had a nightmare, is it?"

The boy shook his head, slowly.

"So, there you are then. No more nonsense, eh?" And with that, she hurried out of the room to put out his breakfast, still chuckling to herself.

The boy sat on his bed, thinking hard. He looked at the empty window sill. He looked at the photograph of his father. Yes, Grandmother was right. Of course she was. It had been a dream after all.

Just to make quite sure he decided to take a quick look at the trunk. He opened the cupboard, and there it was: the big canvas trunk with the leather straps, covered with dust and cobwebs. It couldn't have been touched for years and years.

"I'll just open it, to make quite sure," he said to himself. And he pulled the trunk onto the floor and opened the lid to see what was really inside. Because if last night had been a dream, and if he had not opened the trunk before, then he could not possibly know, could he?

But he did. When he looked inside the trunk he recognized every single thing in it! There were all the toys: the rag doll with one eye, the wind-up train, the Mr. Punch puppet, the money box, and lying on top, the pretty wooden box with the ships painted on its sides! So he must have looked inside the trunk after all! So it could not have been a dream!

"Unless . . . unless . . ." he thought, trying to work it out. "Unless I opened the trunk and *then* I went to sleep, on the floor (that's right, because I was on the floor when I woke up) and I dreamed the rest, about Father and the ghost-boy."

He opened the box and looked inside for the sailor doll. But no, the box was empty. At least . . . he felt around, and drew out a scrap of paper. He unfolded it. It was covered with strange old-fashioned writing.

"The message the ghost-boy wrote," he muttered. "He took away the sailor doll and put this in. I remember now. So there *was* a ghost-boy . . . Oh dear!" And by now he was beginning to feel frightened again. He began to read the scrap of paper. The ghost-boy's message seemed to be a kind of poem.

"Once upon a time there was a dark, dark Wood," he read.

"And in the dark, dark Wood there was a dark, dark House."

"Oh, *no!*" He slammed the paper down fast. "Not *that* again."

As he spoke, the soft far away voices of Grandmother, Father, and the ghost-boy seemed to float into the room, saying the poem all together.

"And in the dark, dark House there was a dark, dark Hall,

And in the dark, dark Hall there were some dark, dark Stairs ..."

"Stop it! Stop it!" cried the boy.

But the voices went on and on, getting louder and louder and faster and faster.

"And in the dark, dark Room there was a dark, dark Corner,

And in the dark, dark Corner there was a dark, dark Cupboard.

And in the dark, dark Cupboard there was a dark, dark Trunk,

And in the dark, dark Trunk there was a dark, dark Box!"

The three voices laughed and laughed before they went on:

"And in the dark, dark Box there was a SILLY POEM,

And the silly poem said:

'Once upon a time there was a dark, dark Wood and ...'"

The boy could bear it no longer. He seized the scrap of paper and tore it into tiny pieces and threw the pieces into the trunk with the pretty wooden box. Then he slammed down the lid, and threw the trunk into the back of the cupboard, and shut the door tight.

At once the voices stopped.

"There. That's shut you up," the boy shouted into the cupboard. "And I don't care what anyone says. Granny *is* right. You were just a dream. And anyway, I don't believe in ghosts!" He ran out of the room and down the stairs to have his breakfast.

And the bedroom was quiet and peaceful, just as a bedroom should be. And the picture of Father stared

unwinkingly out from its frame, just as a picture should. And the old trunk sat in the cupboard, covered with dust and cobwebs, just as it had for twenty years.

And the sun shone through the window.

And on the window sill stood the little wooden sailor doll.

And he winked.

THE FRAID

Susan Price

Once upon a time, on that hot, green island called Jamaica, where monkeys live in the trees, there lived a little girl named Anil, with her mother. They lived a good many miles from anywhere, so Anil had no one to play with, and one day she said to her mother, "Can I go down the road and play with the little boy who lives there?"

"Yes," said her mother, "but mind you come back before it's dark." And she wagged her finger at Anil, the way mothers do. Up in the trees, the monkeys saw what she did and they all wagged their fingers at each other. Because monkeys always copy what they see people doing.

"Why do I have to come back before it's dark, Mother?" asked Anil.

"Because if you come home when it's dark, you'll be afraid."

"What's a Fraid, Mother?" asked Anil, but her

mother only said,

"If you come home in the dark you'll know what afraid is."

Anil went off down the road, and the monkeys followed her, jumping through the trees. She walked a long way to the neighbour's house, and spent all day playing with the little boy who lived there. They held hands and danced in a circle, singing, "Ring-a-ring-a-roses," and the monkeys copied them, except that the monkeys held tails instead of hands. Monkeys always copy what they see people doing.

When the neighbour's little boy was put to bed Anil started home – but it was already dark, and when she got home, her mother was very angry.

"Where have you been?" she shouted. "Didn't I tell you to come home before dark? Didn't I tell you?" She was so angry, she shook her fist; and all the monkeys in the trees shook their fists too.

"But Mother, I'm not a Fraid," said Anil.

"If you walk about in the dark, you'll be afraid," said her mother. "You're not to do it. You're to come home before it gets dark, do you hear?"

Well, a few days later Anil was lonely again, and said to her mother, "Mother, can I go down the road and play with the little boy there?"

"Do you promise to come home before dark?" asked her mother.

"Yes, I promise," said Anil.

"Then you can go. But remember what I said."

So Anil went off down the road, to the neighbour's house there, and she spent all day playing with the little boy who lived there. They played hide and seek, covering their eyes with their hands. The monkeys copied, but sometimes they covered their eyes with their hands and sometimes they covered their eyes with their tails. But monkeys always copy.

Anil enjoyed herself so much that she forgot what she'd promised her mother, and it was dark again before the started home.

Her mother was furious. "You came home in the dark again!" she shouted and jumped in the air, she was so angry. Up in the trees, all the monkeys jumped and shouted too.

"I'm sorry, Mother," Anil said. "But, you see, I'm not a Fraid."

"But you will be afraid," said her mother. "You will be, you'll see, if you don't learn to come home before it gets dark."

A few days after that, Anil said to her mother, "Mother, can I go down the road again, to play with the little boy there?"

"Yes, but what do I want you to do?"

"You want me to come home before dark, Mother."

"And why?"

"Because I'll be a Fraid if I don't."

"That's right," said her mother. "Remember, this time."

So off Anil went. But she enjoyed playing with

the neighbour's little boy too much, and she forgot all about going home before dark. They played one more game, and one more – and it was dark before Anil noticed.

When her mother saw that it was already dark, and that Anil hadn't come home yet, she thought: I'll teach that little girl of mine a lesson that she won't forget. I'll make her afraid, she thought. Then she'll remember to come home where it's safe before it gets dark.

So, she went into the house, and she got a large white sheet from a bed. The monkeys leaned down

from the trees, and they hung on the edge of the roof, and they looked into the house and watched her. And one brave monkey went into the house, and got a little white towel. It was copying Anil's mother, because monkey's always copy what they see people doing.

Anil's mother took the sheet and she went out to the road that Anil would come walking along, and she hid by the side of the road. And the monkey with the towel hid close by her, because it was copying her.

Anil came walking along the road, not at all afraid, because she didn't know what afraid was. And when her mother saw her coming, she put the big white sheet over her head, so that she would look like a ghost. And the monkey copied her. It put the white towel over its head.

When Anil came close, her mother stood up and made the sheet flap, and she went, "Whooo! Whoooooo!" so she would sound like a ghost. And Anil saw this strange white flapping thing in the dark, making this strange noise, and she thought, What can this be? I know! It must be that thing that Mother told me about – it must be a Fraid!

But the monkey was still copying her mother. Behind her, the monkey stood up with the towel over its head, and it flapped its arms and made whooping noises as monkeys do.

"Oh, look!" said Anil, "There's another Fraid! There's a little Fraid! Look behind you, Big Fraid, there's a Little Fraid behind you!"

And her mother did turn around and look behind her, and when she saw the little monkey flapping its sheet and whooping, she thought it was a *real* ghost. And she was so afraid that she ran away! Up the road she ran, to get away from the little ghost.

But, because the monkey was copying everything she did, the monkey ran after her, still with the towel over its head.

"Oh Big Fraid!" shouted Anil, "Little Fraid's after you! Run Big Fraid, Little Fraid's after you!"

And Anil's mother ran and ran, until the monkey's towel fell off, and she saw it was only a monkey. And then she felt silly.

And that's the end of this story and, as far as I know, Anil never did learn what afraid was.

THE HOUSE THAT LACKED A BOGLE

Sorche Nic Leodhas

There once was a house that lacked a bogle. That would be no great thing for a house to be wanting in the ordinary way, but it happened that this house was in St Andrews. That being a town where every one of the best houses has a ghost or a bogle, as they call it, of its own, or maybe two or even more, the folk who lived in the house felt the lack sorely. They were terribly ashamed when their friends talked about their bogles, seeing that they had none of their own.

The worst of it was that they had but lately come into money and had bought the house to set themselves up in the world. They never thought to ask if it had a bogle when they bought it, just taking it for granted that it had. But what good was it to be having a fine big house if there was no bogle in it? In St Andrews, anyway!

The man of the house could be reckoned a warm

man with a tidy lot of money at his banker's, while his neighbour MacParlan had a hard time of it scraping enough to barely get by. But the Mac-Parlans had a bogle that had been in the family since the time of King Kenneth the First, and they had papers to prove it.

The woman of the house had two horses to her carriage and Mrs MacNair had no carriage at all. But the MacNairs had *three* bogles, being well supplied, and Mrs MacNair was so set up about them that it fair put one's teeth on edge to hear her going on about them and their doings.

Tammas, the son of the house, told his parents that he couldn't hold up his head when chaps talked about their bogles at his school, and he had to admit that there weren't any at his house at all.

And then there was Jeannette, the daughter of the house, (her name was really Janet but she didn't like the sound of it, it being so plain). Well, *she* came home one day, and banged the door to, and burst into tears. And when they all asked her what was amiss, she said she'd been humiliated entirely because they hadn't a bogle, and she'd never show her face outside the house again until her papa got one for her.

Well, it all came to this. Without a bogle, they could cut no figure at all in society, for all their money.

46

They did what they could, of course, to set the matter right. In fact, each one of them tried in his or her own way, but not letting on to the others, lest they be disappointed if naught came of it.

The man of the house kept an eye on MacParlan's house and found out that MacParlan's bogle liked to take a stroll by nights on the leads of MacParlan's roof. So one night, when all the MacParlans had gone off somewhere away from home, he went over and called up to MacParlan's bogle. After a bit of havering, the man got down to the point. "Do you not get terrible tired of haunting the same old place day in and day out?" he asked.

"What way would I be doing that?" the bogle asked, very much surprised.

"Och, 'twas just a thought I had," said the man. "You might be liking to visit elsewhere maybe?"

"That I would not," said the bogle flatly.

"Och well," said the man, "should you e'er feel

the need o' a change of scene, you'll find a warm welcome at my house any time and for as long as you're liking to stay."

The bogle peered down at him over the edge of the roof.

"Thank you kindly," said he, "but I'll bide here wi' my own folks. So dinna expect me." And with that he disappeared.

So there was naught for the man to do but go back home.

The woman of the house managed to get herself asked to the MacNairs' house for tea. She took with her a note to the MacNairs' bogles, telling them she was sure the three of them must be a bit cramped for room, what with there being so many of them and the MacNairs' house being so small. So she invited any or all of them to come over and stay at her house, where they'd find plenty of room and every comfort provided that a bogle could ever wish.

When nobody was watching, she slipped the note down behind the wainscoting in the MacNairs' drawing room, where she was sure the MacNairs' bogles would be finding it.

The MacNairs' bogles found it all right, and it surprised them. They didn't know exactly what to make of the note when they'd read it. But there was no doubt the woman meant it kindly, they said to each other. Being very polite bogles, they decided that she deserved the courtesy of an answer to the note, and since none of them was very much for writing, the least they could do was to send one of themselves to decline the invitation. The woman had paid them a call, so to speak. So one of them went to attend to it that same night.

The bogle met up with the woman of the house just as she was coming out of the linen press with a

pile of fresh towels in her arms. The maids had left that day, being unwilling to remain in a house so inferior that it had no bogle to it. She'd have been startled out of her wits had she not been so glad to see the bogle.

"Och then!" said she, "'tis welcome you are entirely!"

"Thank ye kindly," said the bogle.

"You'll be stopping here I hope?" questioned the woman eagerly.

"I'm sorry to be disappointing you," said the bogle, "but I'm not staying. I'm needed at home."

"Och now," said the woman, "and could they not make do without you just for a month or two? Or happen even a fortnight?"

But she could see for herself that the bogle was not to be persuaded. In fact, none of them could accept her invitation. That's what the bogle had come to tell her. With their thanks, of course.

"'Tis a sore thing," complained the woman, "what with all the money paid out for the house and all, that we have no bogle of our own. Now can you be telling me why?"

"I would not like to say," said the bogle.

But the woman was sure he knew the reason, so she pressed him until at last the bogle said reluctantly, "Well, this is the way of it. The house is too young! Losh! 'Tis not anywhere near a hundred years old yet, and there's not been time enough for anything to have happened that would bring it a bogle of its own. And forbye ..." The bogle stopped talking at that point.

"Och! What more?" urged the woman.

"W-e-e-ell," said the bogle slowly, "I'd not be liking to hurt your feelings, but your family is not, so to speak, distinguished enough. Now you take the MacParlans and the Macphersons and the MacAlistairs – their families go back into the far ages. And the MacAlpines is as old as the hills and rocks and streams. As for the MacNairs," he added proudly, "och, well, the MacNairs *is* the MacNairs. The trouble with your family is that there is nothing of note to it. No one knows exactly where it would be belonging. There's no clan or sept o' the name. Losh! The name has not even a 'Mac' at the front of it."

"Aye," said the woman slowly, "I can see that fine."

And so she could. For the truth was that they had come from Wigtown and were not a Highland family at all.

"Well," said the bogle, "that's the way it is. So I'll bid you good-night." And away he went like a drift of mist, leaving the poor woman of the house alone and uncomforted.

The daughter of the house had taken to her bed and spent her time there, weeping and sleeping, when she wasn't eating sweeties out of a pink satin box and reading romantic tales about lovely ladies who had adventures in castles just teeming with ghosts and handsome gentlemen in velvet suits.

So there was no one left to have a try but the son, Tammas. It must be admitted he did the best he

could, even if it turned out that he was maybe a little bit too successful.

Tammas had got to the place where he kept out of the way of his friends on account of the shame that was on the family; he being young and full of pride. He only went out by night, taking long walks in lonely places all by himself.

One night he was coming back from one of these walks, and he came along by a kirkyard. It was just the sort of spot that suited his gloomy thoughts, so he stopped and leaned over the wall to look at the long rows of gravestones.

"All those graves lying there," he thought, "with many a bogle from them stravaging through the town and not a one of them for us. 'Tis not fair on us."

He stopped to think about the injustice of it, and then he said out loud, "If there's a bogle among you all who's got no family of his own, let him come along with me. He can bide with us and welcome."

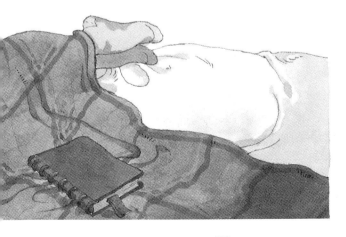

And with a long, deep sigh he turned back up the road and started for home.

He'd not gone more than twenty paces past the end of the kirkyard, when of a sudden he heard a fearful noise behind him. It was so eerie that it near raised the hair right off from his head. It sounded like a cat yowling and a pig squealing and a horse neighing and an ox bellowing all at one and the same time.

Tammas scarcely dared turn and look, with the fright that was on him, but turn he did. And he saw 'twas a man coming toward him. He was dressed in Highland dress with kilt and sporran, jacket and plaid showing plain, and the moonlight glinting off his brooch and shoe buckles and off the handle of the dirk in his hose. He carried a pair of bagpipes under his arm and that was where the noise was coming from.

"Whisht, man," called Tammas, "leave off with the pipes now. The racket you're making's enough to wake the dead."

"'Twill do no such thing," said the piper. "For they're all awake already and about their business. As they should be, it being midnight."

And he put his mouth at the pipes to give another blow.

"Och, then ye'll wake all the folks in St Andrews," protested Tammas. "Give over now, that's a good lad!"

"Och nay," said the piper soothingly. "St Andrews folk will pay us no heed. They're used to us. They even like us."

By this time he had come up to Tammas where he stood in the middle of the road. Tammas took another look at him to see who the piper was. And losh, 'twas no man at all. 'Twas a bogle!

"'Tis a strangely queer thing," said the piper sadly. "I've been blowin' on these things all the days of my mortal life till I plain blew the life out o' my body doing it. And I've been blowing on them two or three hundred years since then, and I just cannot learn how to play a tune on them."

"Well, go and blow somewhere else," Tammas told him. "Where it's lonely, with none to hear you."

"I'd not be liking that at all," said the piper. "Besides, I'm coming with you."

"With me!" Tammas cried in alarm.

"Och aye," said the piper, and then he added reproachfully, "you asked me, you know. Did you not?"

"I suppose I did," Tammas admitted reluctantly. "But I'd no idea there'd be anyone there listening."

"Well, *I* was there," the piper said, "and I was listening. I don't doubt that I'm the only bogle in the place without a family of my own. So I accept the invitation, and thank ye kindly. Let's be on our way."

And off he stepped, with his kilt swinging and his arms squared just so and the pipes going at full blast.

Tammas went along with him, because there was nowhere else he could go at that hour but back to his home.

When they got home, Tammas opened the door and into the house the two of them went. All the family came running to see what was up, for the pipes sounded worse indoors than out since there was less room there for the horrible noise to spread.

"There!" Tammas shouted at them all, raising his

voice over the racket of the bagpipes. "There's your bogle for you, and I hope you're satisfied!"

And he stamped up the stairs and into his room, where he went to bed with his pillow pulled over his ears.

Strange to tell, they really were satisfied, because now they had a bogle and could hold their own when they went out into society. Quite nicely as it happened, for they had the distinction of being the only family in the town that had a piping ghost – even if he didn't know how to play the pipes.

It all turned out very well, after all. The daughter of the house married one of the sons of the MacNairs and changed her name back to Janet, her husband liking it

better. And she had a "Mac" at the front of her name at last, as well as her share of the three MacNair bogles, so she was perfectly happy.

The mother and father grew a bit deaf with age, and the piping didn't trouble them at all.

But Tammas decided he'd had all he wanted of bogles and of St Andrews as well. So he went off to London where he made his fortune and became a real English Sassenach. In time, he even got a "Sir" before his name, which gave him a lot more pleasure than he'd ever have got from a "Mac."

The bogle never did learn to play the bagpipes, though he never left off trying. But nobody cared about that at all. Not even the bogle.

TEENY-TINY

An English tale
retold by Joseph Jacobs

Once upon a time there was a teeny-tiny woman who lived in a teeny-tiny house in a teeny-tiny village. Now, one day this teeny-tiny woman put on her teeny-tiny bonnet, and went out of her teeny-tiny house to take a teeny-tiny walk. And when this teeny-tiny woman had gone a teeny-tiny way, she came to a teeny-tiny gate; so the teeny-tiny woman opened the teeny-tiny gate, and went into a teeny-tiny churchyard. And when this teeny-tiny woman had got into the teeny-tiny churchyard, she saw a teeny-tiny bone on a teeny-tiny grave, and the teeny-tiny woman said to her teeny-tiny self, "This teeny-tiny bone will make me some teeny-tiny soup for my teeny-tiny supper." So the teeny-tiny woman put the teeny-tiny bone into her teeny-tiny pocket, and went home to her teeny-tiny house.

Now, when the teeny-tiny woman got home to her teeny-tiny house, she was a teeny-tiny bit tired; so she went up her teeny-tiny stairs to her teeny-tiny bed, and put the teeny-tiny bone into a teeny-tiny cupboard. And when this teeny-tiny woman had been to sleep a teeny-tiny time, she was awakened by a teeny-tiny voice from the teeny-tiny cupboard, which said:

"Give me my bone!"

The teeny-tiny woman was a teeny-tiny bit frightened, so she hid her teeny-tiny head under the teeny-tiny clothes and went to sleep again. And when she had been to sleep again a teeny-tiny time, the teeny-tiny voice again cried out from the teeny-tiny cupboard and a teeny-tiny bit louder:

"Give me my bone!"

This made the teeny-tiny woman a teeny-tiny bit more frightened, so she hid her teeny-tiny head a teeny-tiny bit further under the teeny-tiny clothes. And when the teeny-tiny woman had been to sleep again a teeny-tiny time, the teeny-tiny voice from the teeny-tiny cupboard said again a teeny-tiny bit louder:

"Give me my bone!"

And this teeny-tiny woman was a teeny-tiny bit more frightened, but she put her teeny-tiny head out of the teeny-tiny clothes, and said in her loudest teeny-tiny voice, "**TAKE IT!**"

THE GHOST TRAIN

Sydney J. Bounds

Billy Trent ran down the lane towards the common, sandy hair poking like straws from under his cap, eyes gleaming with excitement. The common blazed with coloured lights, post-box red and dandelion yellow and neon blue. The evening air throbbed with the sound of fairground music and his pulse beat in rhythm.

He reached the entrance and passed beneath a banner that read:

BIGGEST TRAVELING FAIR IN BRITAIN!

A jolly, red-faced man dressed as a clown called to him. "On your own, son? Enjoy all the fun of the fair."

Billy nodded eagerly, too excited to speak, for the fair came only once a year and he'd saved hard for the occasion. Almost a pound's worth of change clutched tight in his pocket, he darted between the coconut shy and a hamburger stand, chair-o-planes and swing-boats. He paused, fascinated, in front of the carousel with its pairs of magnificent horses going round and round and up and down. He stared up in awe at the big Ferris Wheel revolving in the sky, trying to make up his mind which to try first.

There were dodgem cars, and a snaky switchback ride. Music played, fireworks exploded in cascading showers of light. The smell of cotton candy tempted him. For Billy it was the best night of the year, until . . .

In a shadowy empty space behind the fortune teller's tent, he found himself between two youths dressed in jeans and leather jackets studded with stars.

The big one with the scarred face gripped Billy's arm. "Hi, kid, we'll give you a break – you can pal up with us tonight. It's more fun sharing things. I'm Ed, and my mate here answers to Higgy."

Higgy, fat and pimply, sniggered in a way that gave Billy gooseflesh. "Hi, pal, glad to meet yuh. Ed and me's broke, and that ain't much fun, so I hope you've got plenty of cash. We're all pals together, see?"

Billy shook his head, mute. He had a sinking feeling in his stomach and his hand tightened around the coins in his pocket as he stared up at the two older boys. He decided he didn't like either of them.

Ed's big hand tightened on his arm till it throbbed

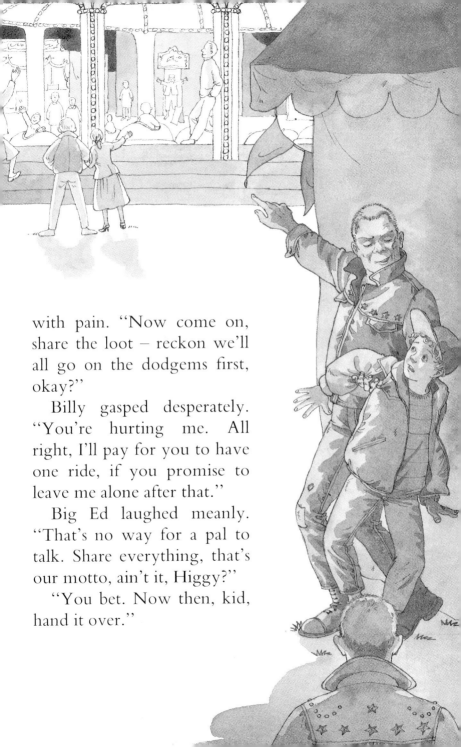

with pain. "Now come on, share the loot – reckon we'll all go on the dodgems first, okay?"

Billy gasped desperately. "You're hurting me. All right, I'll pay for you to have one ride, if you promise to leave me alone after that."

Big Ed laughed meanly. "That's no way for a pal to talk. Share everything, that's our motto, ain't it, Higgy?"

"You bet. Now then, kid, hand it over."

As Billy slowly brought his hand from his pocket, Ed relaxed a fraction, grinning at Higgy. Instantly Billy twisted like an eel, slipped from Ed's grasp and ran off as hard as he could go.

"Little perisher," Ed shouted angrily. "Just wait till I get my hands on 'im – I'll break 'is flaming neck!" With Higgy at his heels, he gave chase.

Billy pushed his way into the fairground crowd, panting, looking for someone – anyone – he knew. But they were all strangers, intent on enjoying themselves and oblivious to his trouble. The music blared loudly and bright colored lights flashed.

Billy glanced back; the two youths were still after him, and Ed's scarred face looked savage. He ran behind a wooden hoarding and found himself trapped between the Wall of Death and the switchback ride. It was dark and he could see no way out. The roar of motor-cycle engines was deafening; even if he shouted, no one would hear. He hunted for somewhere to hide as Ed and Higgy turned the corner and spotted him.

Dim blue lights spelled out:

GHOST TRAIN

Billy could just make out the shape of a miniature steam engine with six open cars in the gloom. The cars were empty. There seemed to be no one about, not even at the pay desk.

As the train began to move towards the dark

mouth of the entrance tunnel, Billy ran forward and sprang into the car nearest the engine. He crouched low, but ...

"There he is!" Ed shouted, pointing. Higgy right behind him, he put on a spurt and they reached the train in time to scramble aboard the last car.

The Ghost Train gathered speed as it rumbled into the tunnel. In the darkness, Billy gulped as he looked up to see the luminous skeleton-figure of the engine driver grinning back at him. But he was too scared of his pursuers to be really frightened.

Then Ed and Higgy started to climb over the empty cars toward him.

The track wound and the cars swayed and rattled. Cobwebs brushed Billy's face. An eerie green glow illuminated the tunnel and a tombstone beside the track; the stone lifted and a cowled figure rose with a dreadful wail.

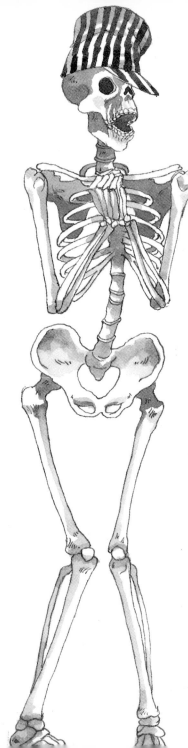

It was night-black again and a woman's scream echoed. In a phosphorescent glow, a headless phantom stalked towards the engine, vanished. Chains clanked and something evil-smelling dripped from the roof. A bat-thing swooped, hissing.

The dark came again. Then a lightning flash revealed a fanged monster.

The train rattled on through the blackness. A red glow from a fire showed three witches stooped over a cauldron; as the train passed, the nearest lifted her death's-head and cackled with laughter.

Suddenly Billy was aware that the two bullies were no longer interested in him. The skeleton-

68

driver of the Ghost Train had left his engine and was moving steadily back along the cars toward them. Ed's face had lost its savage look. Higgy's eyes no longer gleamed with malice.

As a bony arm extended, skeletal finger pointing, they backed away. Empty eye-sockets stared sightlessly at them, jaws gaped in a toothless snarl. A hollow voice intoned: "Beware!" And, scared stiff, Ed and Higgy scrambled back to the last carriage.

The ride ended and Billy got away smartly. As he mingled with the crowd, he saw Ed and Higgy – their faces as white as chalk – hurrying toward the exit. They'd had enough.

Billy looked again for the Ghost Train, but he could not find it now.

Left alone, he enjoyed all the fun of the fair. He went on one ride after another until he'd spent his money. He was very happy as he turned to go home.

On his way out, the clown called to him again. "What did you like best, son?"

Billy Trent paused and thought. "The Ghost Train," he said.

The clown's jolly red face paled. "But there's no Ghost Train now! Used to be one, with Old Tom driving, dressed all in black with a skeleton painted on. Then one day a youngster fell off the train and Tom dived after him. Killed he was, saving the lad. After the accident, the boss scrapped it – so you must have dreamed that."

But Billy was quite sure he hadn't.

A STORY
ABOUT DEATH

Judith Gorog

It was a Tuesday morning in spring when Death walked in our kitchen door. Mama was taking cookies out of the oven. I was sitting on the floor of the pantry, in my special place, drawing and feeling a little sad. Mama was annoyed with me for leaving my baby brother asleep on the big bed in the playroom. He was lying in the middle of the bed with our stuffed animals around him and a big pile of clean laundry at the foot of the bed. He couldn't roll off, but Mama says we might forget he is there in the middle of that mess, and do a somersault on him. True, my sister and I usually do somersaults on that bed.

Death didn't even knock. The door opened and I smelled a basement smell and felt cold air all around me. He didn't see me. He just looked at the cookies on the table and at the cake Mama had just frosted. He looked and looked at that cake. I looked and looked at him. He was just like the pictures of him in books: yellowish-white bones in a long brown robe. The hood was pulled up so that you could hardly see his head. He looked up from the cake at Mama.

"I've come for one of your children. You have three." He held up his bony fingers and counted, "One seven-year-old, one five-year-old, and one baby two months old. Which will it be?"

Mama stopped taking cookies off the cookie sheet. She didn't even look scared. "Must it be one of the children? How about me?"

"How about me!" mimicked Death in a high, mean voice. "Aw. You parents are all the same. No. I have my orders. It must be a child, by twelve noon, so make up your mind. I'm late."

Mama didn't answer him. Was she mad enough to give me to him? I wanted to run to her, but I stayed very still, like a little animal in the forest. I made myself as small as I could and waited to hear what Mama would say. But Mama still didn't answer, just poured a mug of tea for Death and then one for herself. She passed a plate of cookies to Death, then took a sip of her tea. Death ate six cookies in a flash. I have never seen anyone so greedy. Mama poured some milk into her tea. She drank slowly, with

a serious face. I could hardly sit still. Death helped himself to another six cookies.

The kitchen clock hummed. Death crunched his cookies and slurped his tea. Finally Mama said, very slowly, with sips of tea in between, "I have read somewhere that you like games."

"No. No. No games. Those days are over."

"And must it be today?" continued Mama, as if Death had not interrupted her.

"Well," said Death, with a mouthful of cookie. "I must do my job by noon."

Mama got a big knife and cut a large slice of cake, put it on a plate, and got out a fork. Then she offered the plate of cake to Death.

Taking the plate, Death said, "If I don't get one today, I have two more chances."

Mama looked interested. "The children are so young. If you don't get one now, then all of them get to grow very old, to be truly ready for you?"

"Well, yes. I get three tries this time. But I won't miss. No tricks. I'm watching the clock. Well. Which one?" He mumbled because his mouth was full of cake.

Mama took a deep breath. "I'm thinking."

The clock said one minute to twelve.

"Hurry, woman!" gasped Death, nearly choking on his cake. The plate clattered to the kitchen table. As he stood up, all kinds of crumbs fell from his robe to the kitchen floor.

"I suppose it must be the baby," whispered Mama. Her back was to me and I saw that she had her fingers crossed behind her back as she spoke. I nearly cried out.

Death raced upstairs. "He's not in his bed!" he yelled.

"Oh," said Mama. "Where can he be?"

She looked at me and put her finger to her lips, then got out the broom and began to sweep up the crumbs.

Death raced downstairs and out the front door to look in the baby carriage under the cherry tree. It was empty. Then he looked in the baby's bouncy chair.

Twelve was striking on the church clock. I counted under my breath. Eleven. Twelve.

Death slammed out of the kitchen door. "I'll be back tomorrow," he called over his shoulder, and was gone.

Mama and I raced upstairs. The baby was safe, asleep under a large fuzzy bear, the one I've slept with since I was two.

"Mama, what will you do?" I asked.

Mama gave me a big hug. "I'm thinking. With the baby it may just be possible to trick him two more times."

All afternoon Mama was very quiet. She made me promise not to tell what had happened. "I'm not sure that we can trust Death, so be very quiet, and I'll think."

I begged not to go to school the next day, but Mama said that I was over my cold and that I would be safer at school in case her trick should fail.

That night when dinner was over, Mama left us reading with Papa and went out. She came back later with a shopping bag full of something that looked like boxes. We asked if she had been shopping, and she said no, she had been to friends borrowing.

Late that night I thought I heard the baby crying, but when I got up to look, he was quietly asleep in his bed.

Mama made me go to school, but I crept back home just before noon. Death was there, in the kitchen. The whole house smelled delicious. Mama had made a big kettle of soup. Death was just finishing a bowl of it.

"I was angry with you yesterday," he said, "but you are a wonderful cook." He held out his bowl for a second helping, then ate it rapidly, spilling some on his robe. "However," he continued between spoonfuls, "you must learn to accept things."

He held out his bowl for another helping. "Who would leave a baby on a bed full of stuffed animals and clean laundry anyway! He might fall off!" He put down his spoon. "I hear the baby crying now. I'll just go get him."

Mama looked stern. "It's rude to ask for thirds and not to finish."

Death finished his soup quickly and headed out the kitchen door. The crying came from the study. Death ran in. No baby, just a tape recorder playing a tape of my little sister crying when she was a baby.

Then we heard another cry. "Wa-a-a! Wa-a-a!" Death raced up to the baby's bed. Another tape recorder. "Not here!" yelled Death. "Wait. I'll smell him out." But when he sniffed, the whole house was full of the smell of the soup. "Wa-a-a," came another long cry from the guest bedroom. But there was another tape recorder. In every room a tape recorder played the calls and cries of babies. Death raced from room to room, his robe flapping. His voice was angrier and angrier. My heart was pounding as I began to count the strokes of the church clock. I could hardly hear it for all of the babies crying . . . six . . . seven . . . eight . . . nine . . . ten . . . eleven . . . . . . twelve.

"You think you're so smart," Death snarled at Mama. "Tomorrow I won't miss."

He slammed the back door. Mama went through the house turning off recorders. Just then the baby awoke and began to call. "Aya, aya, aya." I ran to the pantry. My baby brother was on top of the refrigerator on a bed of clean diapers and towels in his plastic baby bathtub.

As Mama fed the baby, she began to cry. She didn't even scold me for coming home to spy.

"Mama, what will you do now?" I asked as I stroked the baby's fuzzy head. He stopped eating to grin at me. He has no teeth, so it is all gums and drool when he smiles.

"He has only one more try," said Mama.

The next day I had just managed to sneak home and hide when Death arrived. He was early. Mama was holding the baby in her arms when Death walked in the door. On the kitchen table were three loaves of freshly baked bread, a full butter dish, and a big bread knife. On the sideboard was a large fat hen Mama was planning to roast for dinner.

Death helped himself to bread and butter. "I'm glad you are going to be reasonable," he said.

"May I just feed him first?" asked Mama softly.

My baby brother gurgled and cooed in her arms. Then he began to chew his fist. "Oh. All right, but no more delay. I can't stand about nattering all day with you. I have work to do," Death complained. He cut another slice of bread and spread the butter on it from edge to edge very carefully before he took a big bite.

Mama wrapped the baby in a big blue flannel blanket and sat down in the kitchen armchair to nurse. Death poured himself a mug of tea and took another slice of bread and butter.

It was nearly twelve when Mama began to burp the baby. The telephone rang. "Answer that, will you please?" Mama said to Death. Death went to the telephone in the front hall.

The baby burped a big one.

Death held the receiver against his chest and leaned around the kitchen door. "It's a carpet-cleaning service. They have a special on this week. Do you want the carpets cleaned?"

"No, thank you," said Mama, as she put the baby to the other breast.

The church clock began to strike twelve. Death slammed down the telephone and ran into the kitchen. "No more fooling!" he said as he snatched the bundle from Mama's arms and rushed out the back door. Mama hid her face in her hands.

The clock was silent. Then we heard Death's angry wail. "Cheat! Che-e-e-eat!" he cried. But he didn't come back.

Mama looked up and gave a great big sigh. "He's gone."

Very slowly she leaned over to reach under the table. She lifted the towel that covered the big bowl we use for making bread. There was my baby brother, chewing on his fist. I couldn't believe my eyes.

"Mama. I didn't see you do that," I said.

Mama pointed to the sideboard, and then picked up my baby brother. I looked to where she pointed and began to laugh and jump up and down. The fat hen was gone.

"Yug-g-g, Mama," I said. "You held that cold thing to your breast!"

SHIVER AND SHAKE

Grimm Brothers
retold by Amabel Williams-Ellis

Long, long ago, there were two brothers. Their father always said what a clever boy the elder one was. As for the younger brother, whose name was Fritz, the father treated him as if he were nothing more or less than a Silly.

Now though the elder brother really was a sharp, sensible fellow, there was just one thing that, even when he was quite grown up, the elder brother didn't like. He didn't like going through the churchyard after dark and, if his father wanted him to go out and fetch something, he would always somehow manage to put off going that way until the next morning.

"Going through that churchyard in the dark makes me shiver and shake with fear!" he would say.

The younger son – the one that everyone called Silly – used to sit in the corner listening to his brother when he said this, and he couldn't think what in the world he meant.

"Other people are always saying that sort of thing – it makes me shiver and shake with fear," he would say to himself. "But I don't know anything about shivering and shaking with fear. What can they mean? It's time I learned! What a lot there is that I don't know!"

After a while it was time for the two boys to go out and seek their fortune. The elder son had learned a trade, so that was all right, but Fritz didn't know any trade, so his father asked him what he would like to learn.

"I should like to learn how to shiver and shake – I don't know how to do that at all!" said Fritz.

When his father and elder brother heard that, how they laughed!

"You'll learn soon enough, Silly!" said his father, still laughing and, with that, he gave each of them as much money as he could spare to start them off with.

After they had walked for a while they parted ways, for all Fritz wanted to learn was just this one thing!

"Good luck to you then, Silly! You'll learn that fast enough!" said the elder brother. They shook hands and then each went his way.

Well, after he had journeyed alone for a time, Fritz met a wagoner who was going with his horse and cart to the next town. He went along with him and, as they went, they began to talk and the boy told the wagoner what it was that he wanted to learn.

"Well, you're a Silly indeed!" said the wagoner, laughing. "Never mind, you're a nice boy and I dare say we can find a job for you when we get to the town."

In the evening they came to an inn and the wagoner put his cart in the yard and his horse in the stable, and he and Fritz went to the kitchen. While they were sitting by the fire, the wagoner told the innkeeper, as a good joke, what it was that Fritz wanted to learn. At that the innkeeper laughed just as loudly as his father and brother, and just as merrily as the wagoner.

"If that is all you want, you funny fellow," said the innkeeper, "it'll be easy enough in this town!"

"Oh, husband!" said the innkeeper's wife, who was a kind woman, "Don't tell the boy about that! Too many nice young men have come to grief over it already – it would be a pity if such a good-natured boy as this should lose his life as well as the rest."

So then of course Fritz wanted to know all about it, and he would let the innkeeper have no peace. At last the innkeeper said:

"Not far from here there stands an enchanted castle with a great treasure hidden in it. Whoever can manage to stay three nights in it, all alone, will be able to break the evil spell, and the King has promised that whoever can do this shall marry his daughter and have half his kingdom. The Princess is

the most beautiful maiden that the sun ever shone on. But alas, the castle is guarded by evil spirits, and though many bold young men have tried to stay alone there for three nights, it has always been too much for them. Not one has ever come out alive."

The kind innkeeper's wife would hardly let him finish, but kept telling Fritz that he must not try, but that, instead, they would give him a job helping at the inn. But say what she might it was all no use. Fritz had made up his mind.

So the very next morning off he set for the palace and when he got there he asked to see the King. When he stood before him, Fritz at once asked if he could be the next to try to stay three nights at the enchanted castle. The King looked at him sadly for, like the innkeeper's wife, he thought it was a pity that such a nice-looking boy should die like the others. So he only shook his head and told Fritz that he had better be off, for he would be sure to die of fright like the rest of them. But the lad begged him, saying that he really must be allowed to try.

"Do let me, your Majesty! There's nothing I want so much in the world as to learn how to shiver and shake with fright." At last he begged so hard that the King said:

"Have it your way then!" and then told him the conditions. "You may ask for three things to take into the castle with you," said the King, "but they mustn't, any of them, be alive, for you have to watch there quite alone. What will you take?"

Fritz thought for a while, then he said:

"First, I'll have plenty of firewood and something to kindle it with; second, food and drink; and third, a good strong carving-knife."

So the King agreed that these things could count as three, and ordered his men to bring them to the castle during the day. Then the boy went back to the inn, well pleased, and as he walked, he whistled, and he spent the rest of the day, helping the innkeeper's wife to wash the pots and beer mugs.

When it began to grow dark, off he we[nt to] the enchanted castle. He made himself a g[ood] fire in one of the huge rooms, found a ben[ch] up to the fire, and sat himself down to wait for what would happen. For a while nothing happened at all. But towards midnight something began to cry miserably from one of the corners.

"Meow! Meow! How cold we are!"

"Don't be silly," called out Fritz, "if you're cold, come here and sit by the fire, and warm yourselves."

No sooner had he spoken than two black cats, as big as wolves, that looked at him savagely with their fiery eyes, sprang out of two dark corners and sat down by the fire. No sooner had these fierce cats sat down than, out of every dark place in the huge room, more enormous black cats began to creep out, and soon there were black dogs as well. They all had eyes like coals and the dogs had red-hot chains. More and more of them came, until the room – big

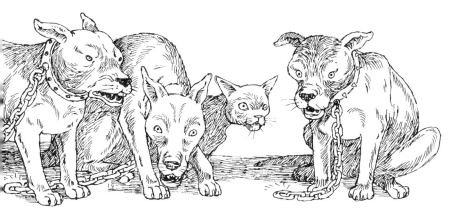

85

ȝ it was — was crowded with them and they all meowed and barked and spat and growled and made a horrible noise. The boy didn't mind all that a bit. But soon the beasts began to paw at the fire and pull it to pieces – this nearly put it out – so that the room began to get much darker. Then Fritz got cross and, standing up and taking the big carving-knife, he called out:

"Away with you!"

But instead of going away they began to snap and claw at him, and so then he began to slash at them. At that, some of them ran away with their tails between their legs, but the others he killed, and, opening a window, he threw their bodies, plop, down into the castle moat. When he had cleared up he made up the fire again and sat down to eat his supper and then toasted himself warm. Presently he went off very comfortably to sleep.

Now the King had taken a liking to Fritz and, all night, he had felt quite worried about him, so next morning he decided to come down himself from his palace to see what had happened. So, as soon as it was light, in came the King and his attendants. There lay Fritz on the ground, so still that the King was sure he must be dead.

"Alas!" said the King sorrowfully. "What a pity! A nice young fellow like that! Dead! In the flower of his youth!"

But just then Fritz sprang to his feet and, when he saw who was there, he bowed politely. The King was astonished and very much pleased.

"What sort of night did you have?" he asked.

"Oh, it went very well indeed!" said the boy and told the King about the monstrous cats and frightful dogs. "But," added he sadly, "I still don't know anything about shivering and shaking! If only someone would show me how!"

The King was delighted but he shook his head when he heard that Fritz meant to try again. However, he went back to his palace, while Fritz went back to the inn. There he spent the day as merrily as before, helping the innkeeper and his wife.

When evening came, Fritz went alone to the castle just as before, and, once again, he made a good fire and sat down on his bench. Everything was quiet until nearly midnight and then, up above, began a terrible noise of thumping and banging. Then suddenly, half a man came tumbling down the chimney into the hearth at his feet!

"Hello!" said the boy, "hello and welcome, but surely there ought to be some more of you?"

Then the noise began again and down fell the other half.

"Poor fellow," said the boy, "you seem to have had a rough journey! Sit down and warm yourself." And with that Fritz got up to make a better fire. When he looked around the two pieces had joined themselves together, and a huge and horribly ugly man was sitting on the bench where he had been.

"No, no," said Fritz, "that bench is mine! That stool is for you."

With that the horrible man began to yell and scream with rage and tried to push Fritz away. But the boy wouldn't allow that, and he forced the horrible man to fetch the stool and sit on it. Then Fritz offered him some of his food and drink, and when they had both had some supper the boy said:

"We ought to play something to pass the time till morning."

"The horrible man did not answer, but, with a sudden yell, he put both his arms up the chimney and brought down a lot of bones and skulls.

"Oh," said the boy, "I see! You want to play a game, and use these skulls as balls."

And so they played, and Fritz was very strict with the horrible man and wouldn't let him cheat, and he took no notice of how he screamed and made faces and how he even tried to strangle Fritz every time he lost. As soon as the first cocks crowed and the light of morning came, the horrible man dropped into two pieces once more, and both halves, with all the skulls and bones, vanished up the chimney.

Once more the King came down in the morning from his palace to see how Fritz had got on.

"I have had a jolly night of it, playing games," said Fritz and he went on to tell the King all that had happened.

"And didn't it make you shiver and shake with fear to play games with such a horrible creature as that?" asked the King.

"Oh dear no," said the lad. "We were very merry, so, alas, I still don't know how to shiver and shake."

Once more Fritz spent the day helping the good innkeeper and his wife, and once more, when it began to grow dark, he went back alone to the enchanted castle.

Now, as you know, Fritz had hardly slept at all that night because he had been playing games nearly all night with the horrible man. So this time, he felt very sleepy. When he had lit his fire he looked around the room and saw something that he had not noticed before. There was a big bed in one corner.

"That bed is just what I want!" he thought, and so in he got and pulled up the bedclothes. He was just settling down comfortably, and his eyes were just shutting with sleep, when, with a terrific gust of wind, the door of the room opened by itself and the bed began moving of its own accord.

Out of the room rolled the bed with Fritz on it, and off it went with him down a dark passage. Bats flew out at him, cold hands grabbed at him, glowing eyes stared at him. As the bed carried him along he could see heaps of treasure that sparkled in the moonlight and each heap was guarded by some monster that was worse than the last.

"This is a grand way to see the castle! Go faster! Go faster!" cried Fritz. At that the bed rolled on at a great pace; indeed it rolled as if six horses were

harnessed up to it. Up and down it bumped all over
the castle, while the wind howled, the moonlight
gleamed on heaps of treasure and on swords that
slashed at him and on bats that flew out at him. Over
thresholds and steps rolled the bed, and even up
winding staircases, until at last, it brought him right
out into the moonlight on to the highest turret of the
castle battlements. Just as the bed seemed to be going
to roll right off the turret with him and plop, down
into the castle moat, the first light of morning began
to colour the sky and the first cocks crew. Then,
with that, the bed stayed still.

"Splendid!" called out the lad. "Well done, bed! But really I still feel too sleepy to move. There are plenty of quilts and blankets here, I shall be comfortable enough," so, without even getting out to have a look, Fritz tucked himself up, turned over and went to sleep, just where he was.

Well, next morning, when the King came to the great room of the castle as before, he found that this time the fire was out, and that there was no sign of the boy. The King began to feel very sorrowful, for he had hoped that, on this last morning, he would surely find him once more. He now had not much hope, but all the same he sadly ordered the soldiers who were with him, to search the castle.

"You may at least find the poor young fellow's dead body," said he.

So off the soldiers went. They went along passages, up winding stairs and down into dungeons – up they went and down they went and could find nothing.

At last one of them came up right out of the castle onto the roof and to the top of the highest turret of all. You can guess how astonished he was to see a bed up there, and the boy in it well tucked up and fast asleep. The soldier rushed down at once and told the King the good news. The King wouldn't believe it at first, so he came up to see for himself, and he was delighted when he found that it was all true, and that there lay the boy fast asleep, just as the soldiers had said.

"Wake up, wake up!" cried the King. "You have broken the enchantment! You are safe and sound, and now you can marry my daughter!"

"Yes, your Majesty," said the boy, sitting up, rubbing his eyes, yawning, and looking around him in surprise, and it wasn't for a moment or two that he remembered to get up and bow to the King. "Marry the Princess! That I will gladly do," he went on, "for they tell me she is the most beautiful Princess that the sun ever shone on, and what's more I shan't come to her as a poor man, for now I know where all these heaps of treasure are hidden. But oh dear! I still don't know what it is to shiver and shake!"

But the King only laughed, took him to the Palace, and, as they went, Fritz told him all his night's adventures. The Princess was waiting for them and she really was more beautiful than any maiden that Fritz had ever seen. He was given grand clothes to wear and, the next day, there was a very splendid wedding, and soon Fritz and his Princess loved each other very much.

But as time went on the Princess noticed that sometimes Fritz looked sad, so, one day, she asked him what was the matter. He told her how he had always wanted to learn how to shiver and shake, and that all his adventures in the enchanted castle hadn't helped him to learn how to do it. The Princess did not answer, but, instead, she thought what she could do to help her husband to get his wish.

It was winter, and the stream that ran through the Palace garden was icy cold. One day, when her young husband sat sadly by the fire, the Princess and her maidens went out secretly. They fetched a bucketful of ice-cold water from the stream and into the bucket they put as many little, cold, wriggling fish as they could catch. Then coming in again, the Princess stole softly behind her husband and, without a word, she emptied the ice-cold water, fish and all, all down his neck and all over him.

"Don't!" he cried, jumping up. "Dear wife, what are you doing! That makes me shiver and shake!"

With that the Princess began to laugh, and all her maidens laughed too, and last of all Fritz laughed, and then he kissed the Princess tenderly.

"Thank you, thank you, dear wife!" said he. "Now, thanks to you, at last I know how to shiver and shake!"

And they lived happily ever after.

THEY WAIT

Jan Mark

I don't like getting up in the dark," Jenny said.

"The clocks go back tomorrow night," Mum said. "The mornings'll be lighter then."

"But the evenings'll be darker," said Mark.

Jenny said, "I don't like going out in the dark with all those little things that squeak."

"Mice?" asked Mum, trying to button up Jenny's coat and not listening properly.

"No, not mice," Jenny said. "They fly."

"Do hold still, Jen."

"You've buttoned a loose bit of my neck into my coat," Jenny complained.

"Well, what do you expect, wriggling about like that?"

"Flying mice," said Mark.

"Bats," said Mum. "That's what you hear at night. You don't want to be afraid of bats."

"Bats *are* flying mice," Mark said. "*I* can't hear

94

them squeak."

"I know they're bats. That button's in the wrong hole," Jenny said. "Can *you* hear them squeak?"

"I'm much too old," said Mum, who usually got quite cross if you thought that she was any kind of old. "But when you're little you can hear all sorts of things that grown-ups can't. Anyway, there aren't any bats at this time of year."

Jenny said, "Can I *see* things that grown-ups can't?"

Mum was getting restless because the hands of the kitchen clock were pointing to half past eight, and you could never be sure with that clock. It might be half past by now, but it could as easily be quarter past, or worse, twenty to nine. She said, "Yes, I expect so, especially you – you're always seeing things. Do get a move on."

"No, I'm not," said Jenny. "Look, you've put your shopping bag on the Major's chair. It's right on his lap."

Mum lifted the basket onto the table. "See what I mean?" she said to Mark, over Jenny's head. Only Jenny could see the Major, and the Other Granny, and Mary Dog. The Major and the Other Granny were obviously people but no one, not even Jenny, was sure about Mary Dog. They had never been able to discover whether she was a person whose name happened to be Dog or a dog whose name happened to be Mary. Whoever she was, she lived under the table and rode a bicycle. The Major sat in a wicker chair and spat out of the window. Other Granny, fortunately, lived outside, in the alley, and never went visiting.

"You'd better hurry," Mum said. "It can't be earlier than quarter past." The clock was very old, and had belonged to Real Granny's granny. Sometimes the hands hurried on the way down hill, rested for a bit at the bottom, and dawdled their way toward the top, so the clock was usually right on the hours, but rarely in between. Mark took Jenny by the mitten and hurried her out.

It was a dull morning, more like January than October, and last night's mist was still hanging about in the alley that led to the bus stop, on the ring road. Mark trotted Jenny along the alley because she would keep stopping to feel sorry for the poor pale roses, with frostbitten petals, that were still growing hopefully through the gaps in Mrs Callaghan's fence. Jenny could be sorry for anything, even plants. Last summer she had taken pity on a poor hydrangea bud that was smaller than any of the others on the bush by the back door. For months she had tried to fatten it up with butter and sugar and juice squeezed out of old tea bags, and when it went black and died she had picked it and buried it on the rockery. There was still a little cross of twigs where it lay next to the poor dead beetles and the poor dead flies.

The alley turned right and ran down hill slightly, between the backs of garages, until it came out into the open air again by Churchfield Garden. This was a little plot in the angle of Union Street and the ring road. It was fenced with flat round-headed stones, and there was a path along the edge with flower beds on either side, and a lawn in the middle, with another path running across that, and a long garden bench for people to sit on. Very few people did sit there, so it would have been a useful place to play. Mark was too old for that, but when Jenny got under her feet Mum often said, "Why don't you go down and play in Churchfield Garden?" but Jenny never would.

"I don't like the people there," she said.

"Has someone been bothering you?" Mum asked, anxiously.

"Oh no, but they aren't nice, those people. There's a little girl with a funny eye, and an old man with one leg, and an old woman with one tooth, and a lady with no head . . ."

"Oh," said Mum. "*Those* sort of people. Well, ask the Major to go with you – he'll see them off."

"The Major doesn't go out," said Jenny. "Anyway, he wouldn't like them either."

Jenny would not even cross the garden by the centre path, as Mark did, even when they were late, so every morning it was Mark who ran cater-corner to wave down the school coach, while Jenny galloped around the long way, on the pavement.

Mark saw her safely on board, waved goodbye, and then stood back to wait for his own transport. He was too old to be allowed a free journey to school. Either he had to catch the service bus, or, if he was lucky, he might get a lift from Tim's dad, if Tim's dad happened along first, in his car. Although the mist had disappeared here, on the edge of town, he could see that it must be still quite thick out in the country, so he was not too worried when he heard the church clock strike the three-quarters. If he were late for school he could blame the National Bus Company. Tim was going to be late, too, but he could only blame his dad and Mark, knowing Tim's dad, thought that probably this was not a very safe thing to do.

The clock that he could hear was in the tower of Holy Cross, several streets away. There had once been another church, closer to hand, but Mark had never seen it. It had stood by the burial ground until it was bombed in 1942, which was why the little park was called Churchfield Garden, and the roads on the council estate were all named after it: St Michael's Close, Church Walk, Rectory Drive, and The Glebe. Jenny and Mark lived in Church Walk, and Mark knew that their house was just about where the east end of the old church had been, St Michael and All Angels. Jenny did not know that, and cared less. She still had not realized that names meant something, and thought that they were just useful noises. If their road had been called Coathanger Walk, or Sock Street, she would not have thought it strange. No one who kept friends with a major who spat in public and a dog that rode a bicycle could think that *anything* was odd. The Other Granny did things too, out in the alley, but Mum would not let Jenny talk about her any more. So, although Jenny passed the garden every day, and had invented all sorts of strange people to live in it, she never realized why it was called Churchfield Garden, and was too young to remember the time when the council workmen had come and moved all the tombstones to the edge of the plot, so that there was room to lay the lawns and the paths.

The bus was very late; perhaps it had hit a sheep out on the road across the common. But Tim's dad was late too. Perhaps the bus had hit Tim's dad. Mark found his feet turning chilly. It was not really a *cold* morning, but that corner always seemed cooler than anywhere else, always in the shadow of the trees that still grew nearby, or the old warehouse on the far side of the ring road. To keep warm he began stamping like a guardsman around the paths of Churchfield Garden, until he heard the bus growling in the distance on the other side of the bridge. Then he ran to meet it at the bus stop, but not until the very last moment. No matter how warm the day, there was always a chilly wind around the bus stop, and that morning it was bitter. Mrs Callaghan and Mrs Carter from next door, who had also come down to catch the bus to work, had walked all the way up to the lamppost to keep warm, and had to run even further than he did.

In the evening Mark usually arrived before

Jenny's coach, because his bus came around by the ring road while the school coach got stuck in the city traffic, so he waited for her, to see her across the busy road, which was kind of him because if she got there first she never waited for him, but crossed the busy road by herself and raced home as fast as she could. To save him waiting for nothing she would go upstairs and flash her bedroom light on and off. As you could see her bedroom window only from the other side of the road, by the bus stop next to Churchfield Garden, he had to cross over to look, although it meant loitering in that mean chill draft and then stepping out like a lollipop man when Jenny arrived.

But tonight, when he got down from the bus and crossed the road to Churchfield Garden, he found that he could not see the window at all. Evidently other people beside himself had complained about the wind, for now, beside the bus stop, stood a new wooden shelter with a bench inside it and a timetable in a red metal frame, screwed to the outside wall. He stood first on the left side, then on the right, but no matter where he stood he could no longer see Jenny's window. After hopping about from one cold foot to the other for ten minutes, he decided that Jenny's coach could not possibly be this late, and if it were it was just too bad, and set off home. Jenny, of course, was there before him, in the living-room, being sorry for a poor doggy on television.

"Don't be," he advised her, "it's the hero. It'll be all right."

"But it's hurt its poor *paws*, and it's lost in the *snow*," Jenny whimpered.

"Yes, but in a minute it'll rescue a poor little orphan who's buried in a snow drift and someone'll give it a medal. You know it will. It happens every week."

"But its paws hurt *now*," Jenny wailed.

"Idiot. It's a film. It's not even a new film. It was made about twenty years ago."

"Do dogs live for twenty years?"

"Not often," he said, un-wisely.

"You mean, it's *dead*?"

Mark gave up and went to find Mum. She was in the kitchen frying sausages.

"Had a good day?" she asked.

"It was all right. Jason sat on my sandwiches at break, but he didn't mean to," Mark said. "There's a new shelter down by the bus stop."

"I know. I saw it when I went into the town for the shopping. They'd just finished putting it up."

"It'll keep the wind off," Mark said. "Did you sit in it? Were you the first? You could have officially opened it – you know; I declare this bus shelter well and truly open and may God bless all who sail in her."

"It doesn't keep the wind off," Mum said. "I did sit in it, and it was even colder inside than it was out. It seems to trap the draft."

Jenny appeared in the doorway, wiping her eyes. "I sat in it," she said, "just to try it out. But it was all damp and shivery, so I came home."

"It can't be damp," Mum said. "It's new."

"It is damp – like the outside toilets at the old school."

The outside toilets at the old school were one of the reasons that the old school had been closed.

There was no wind at all on Monday, but it was very cold. As usual Jenny was only just in time for her coach, and Tim's dad was right behind it, hooting impatiently, although the bus was not late, he was early. Mark hopped into the back seat, next to Tim. As the car and the bus moved off together, Mark glanced out of the window and saw that someone was sitting in the bus shelter, although Mrs Carter and Mrs Callaghan were standing where they usually did, out on the pavement, smacking their gloved hands together to keep warm.

That evening Mark got off the bus and saw Jenny waiting for him on the other side of the road, under the street lamp. He went after her.

"What are you doing here?"

"I didn't want to wait in the dark."

"It's not dark, Dumbo."

"Why's the light on, then?"

"Street lights always come on before it gets dark, don't they?"

"Well, it's lighter under the light than it is *not* under the light," Jenny argued.

"You should have gone straight home," Mark said. "I wouldn't have minded. You've never waited before."

"I didn't want to pass the bus shelter."

"Is there someone hiding behind it?"

"There's a person in it," Jenny said. "A person who doesn't get on the bus."

"Well, there isn't a bus to get on," said Mark. "Not till half past. Come on home now."

"That person was there this morning," Jenny said. "I saw him from the coach window."

"I saw him too," Mark said. "It's not the same person, nitwit."

"It is." Jenny clung to the lamppost. "It's the same person and he doesn't get on the bus."

"There's no one there now," Mark said. "I just walked past it. Come and look." He got Jenny in a kind of friendly half-Nelson and propelled her toward the bus shelter. "Look," he said, poking his head in, and hers too. "It's empty, isn't it?"

Jenny looked unconvinced and stayed on the pavement. Mark waved his arms about. "See? Nobody there."

"Let's go home," Jenny said, tugging him out again. At either end of the shelter was a little glazed window, so that people inside could see if the bus was coming, and as they turned away Mark saw what it must have been that had frightened Jenny. Some kind of warp in the glass twisted the light in such a way that it seemed as if there were a person sitting inside, but he said nothing, because Jenny saw only the things that she believed in, and no one had told her about the refraction of light.

Thursday was market day, and there was always a long line of people waiting for Mark's bus in the mornings. Mark joined the end of it as Jenny's school coach drew away from the curb, and watched Jenny's small face peering through one of the side windows, toward the bus shelter. There was nothing fearsome about the bus shelter now. The day was bright, with a little sharp wind rattling the dry leaves of the trees in Churchfield Garden, and tossing them in handfuls around the feet of the people at the head of the queue, but it was bright enough for the queue to stand on the pavement, and not so cold as to drive them into the bus shelter. The bus shelter was quite empty – even very, very old Mrs Pickles who had rheumatism and ought to have been keeping warm, was standing in the queue – although when the bus came and Mark had settled

into his favourite seat, at the back, he could have sworn as he looked over his shoulder, that he could see the indistinct silhouettes of two people sitting together at one end of the bench inside the shelter.

His class had football that afternoon, Reds against Greens. Greens won by five goals to three and Mark, in the Greens, scored two of those five goals. Feeling bold and buoyant as he got off the bus, he crossed the road in the cloudy evening light to wait for Jenny in the shelter, for already a sneaky drizzle was trickling out of the sky. He had thought, when he saw it from the opposite pavement, that the shelter was empty, but when he crossed the road he was not so sure. Instead of going in and sitting down he sauntered back and forth along the pavement that glistened now in the light from the street lamp, certain that there *was* somebody in it, someone who could be seen only out of the tail of his eye; as if whoever it was waited until he had passed and then leaned out behind him, withdrawing into the shadows again as he turned to come back. The obvious answer was, of course, to go into the bus shelter and look, since it might be someone he knew; someone from the estate, messing around. But it might be some big tough, like Gary Callaghan or Cynthia Carter, so he contented himself with walking past, just once more, and then going to stand under the street light to wait for Jenny. When the school coach arrived, a few minutes later, he did not remain where he was but crossed over again and collected Jenny from the very step of the coach as the door swung open.

Jenny glanced across the road.

"There's a lot of people waiting for the bus," Jenny said.

"Are there?" Mark said, grimly. "Where?"

"In the shelter," Jenny said.

"Then let's stop and watch them get on," said Mark, and together they sheltered from the rain against the wall of the warehouse, and watched the real shelter, the bus shelter, across the street. From this distance he could see quite clearly that there were people in it, but he could not see the people clearly. In spite of the nearby street lamp, and the fact that daylight still lingered in the road, the inside of the shelter was thick with shadows, long solid shadows, that seemed to cast shadows themselves.

The four-thirty bus changed gear on the other side of the bridge, and as it came over the hump its headlights shone full into the bus shelter, and the shadows shrank into the corners, but the bus did not stop, for no one wanted to get off, and no one wanted to get on. When its tail lights had disappeared around the corner, Jenny and Mark could see that the shelter was still full of people.

"Well, they didn't get on the bus," Mark said. "Who *are* they, Jenny?"

"They're the people who don't get on the bus," Jenny said.

"Can you see their faces? I can't."

"Oh yes," Jenny said. "I know who they are – I've seen them before. There's the man with one leg ... and the old woman with one tooth ... and the

little girl with the funny eye . . . and the lady with no head . . ."

Mark turned on her furiously. "You're making it up!" he shouted. "They're the people you used to see in Churchfield Garden!"

"Yes," Jenny said, "and now they're in the bus shelter."

"Come on home," Mark said crossly, and pulled her across the road, just missing a van that came unexpectedly around the corner. He let go of Jenny's hand feeling that it was her fault that they had been nearly run over, and strode along the path that crossed the garden on the corner. To his surprise he found that Jenny was hurrying after him.

"I thought you didn't like crossing the gardens," he snapped.

"It's all right now," Jenny explained. "There's nobody here. They're all in the bus shelter."

"Who are?"

"The people who don't get on the bus."

And they were. The people who *did* get on the bus stayed outside on the pavement, queuing up in the rain and wind and even snow, all through the winter. They said that the shelter was drafty, and that there was a funny smell about it, and wasn't it *damp*? The bus shelter gradually filled up with rubbish and vandals broke the little windows at either end, and scrawled all over the outside walls, and tore the timetable from its mounting. No one ventured to scrawl on the inside walls. When the clean spring sunshine showed it up in all its desolation, people began to complain that it was an eyesore, and one day the council workmen came with a lorry and took it away.

Mark saw that it had gone one afternoon as he waited for Jenny, and wondered what had happened to the people who *didn't* get on the bus. He thought that perhaps the council workmen had taken them away with the shelter, for these days Jenny played quite happily in Churchfield Garden, and the shelter really was not needed any more for the wind seemed to have died down considerably, but after a while strange rumours began to circulate about something funny in the bus station, down near the left luggage office, and people stopped going there at night, if they could avoid it.

THE WIND ON HAUNTED HILL

Ruskin Bond

Who-*whoo-whooo*, cried the wind as it swept down from the Himalayan snows. It hurried over the hills and passes, and hummed and moaned in the tall pines and deodars.

On Haunted Hill there was little to stop the wind – only a few stunted trees and bushes, and the ruins of what had once been a small settlement.

On the slopes of the next hill there was a small village. The people there kept large stones on their tin roofs to prevent them from blowing away. There was nearly always a wind in these parts. Even on sunny days, doors and windows rattled, chimneys choked, clothes blew away.

Three children were standing beside a low stone wall, spreading clothes out to dry. On each garment they placed a rock. Even then the clothes fluttered like flags and pennants. Usha, dark-haired, rose-cheeked, struggled with her grandfather's long loose shirt. She was eleven or twelve; she wasn't sure which, because they didn't bother with birthdays in the village. Her younger brother, Suresh, was doing his best to hold down a bed-sheet, while Binya, Usha's friend and neighbour, who was slightly older, handed them the clothes, one at a time.

Once they were sure everything was on the wall, firmly held down by rocks, they climbed up on the flat stones and sat there for a while, in the wind and the sun, staring across the fields at the ruins on Haunted Hill.

"I'm going to the bazaar today," said Usha.

"I wish I could come too," said Binya. "But I have to help with the cows and the housework. Mother isn't well."

"I can come!" said Suresh. He was always ready to visit the bazaar, which was three miles away on the other side of Haunted Hill.

"No, you can't," said Usha. "You've got to help Grandfather chop wood."

Their father was in the army and was serving in a distant part of the land, and so Suresh and his grandfather were the only men in the house. Suresh was only eight, chubby and almond-eyed.

"Won't you be afraid to come back alone?" asked Binya.

"Why should I be afraid?"

"There are ghosts on the hill, aren't there?"

"I know, but I'll be back before it gets dark. Ghosts don't appear during the day!"

"Are there many ghosts in the ruins?" asked Binya.

"Grandfather says so. He says that many years ago – over fifty years, when he was a boy – English people lived on the hill. That was when their king – his name was King George – was also a king of India. But it was a bad hill, and their houses were always being struck by lightning. They had to move to the next mountain and build again."

"But if they went away, why should there be ghosts there?" persisted Binya.

"Because, Grandfather says, during a great storm, one of the houses was hit by lightning and everyone in it was killed. A whole family."

"Were there any children?"

"There were two – a brother and sister. Grandfather says they used to wave to him when he passed their house on the way to the bazaar. Now Grandfather is old, but he says the children are still small, and sometimes when he is passing through the ruins, just before it gets dark, he sees them playing on the hillside. They still wave to him, he says."

"Isn't he frightened?"

"They're only children. And besides, old people don't mind seeing ghosts!"

Usha set off for the bazaar at two in the afternoon. Grandfather kept a battered old clock on the shelf, which told everyone the time, give or take half an hour! It was about an hour's walk to the bazaar. Usha went through the fields, now turning yellow with flowering mustard, then along the saddle of the hill and up to the ruins. The path went straight through the ruins. Usha knew it well. She went to the bazaar quite often, to do the weekly shopping or to see her aunt who lived in the town.

Wild flowers grew in the crumbling walls. A wild plum tree grew straight out of the floor of what had once been a large hall. Its soft white blossoms had begun to fall. Lizards scuttled over the stones. A whistling-thrush, its deep purple plumage glistening in the soft March sunshine, sat in an empty window-frame and sang its heart out.

Usha hummed to herself, as she stepped lightly along the path. She did not glance into the old rooms that were now like the entrances to caves, half hidden by clumps of sorrel and thorn bushes. She had no wish to explore the ruins – not while she was on her own!

They were soon left behind. The path dipped steeply down to the valley, to the little town with its straggling bazaar.

Usha took her time in the bazaar. It was a bustling, colourful place, where you could spend all day if you weren't in a hurry. Usha didn't have all day, but she wasn't in too much of a hurry. After buying the important things like soap, spices and sugar, a new pipe-stem for her grandfather's hookah, and an exercise book for Suresh to do his sums in, she lingered in front of the shops where the expensive items stood behind glass. There were boxes of sweets, dolls and toys for the richer town children, shawls and Tibetan curios for the tourists; nothing that a village girl could afford. But she still

had a rupee to spare, so she bought a dozen marbles for Suresh.

Then she met Aunt Lakshmi, who was haggling over the price of a cauliflower. Aunt Lakshmi took her home and gave her a pair of pretty glass bangles. In return, Usha had to sit and listen to her aunt talk about the ache in her left shoulder and the stiffness in her right knee. When she looked out of the window, she saw that great dark clouds had gathered over the hills.

"I must go," she said. "Thank you, Aunt Lakshmi. I'll come again soon, with cauliflowers grown at home."

Her shopping bag was full. She slung it over her

shoulder and set out for home. Oddly enough, the wind had dropped. The trees were still, not a leaf moved. The crickets were silent in the grass. The crows flew around in circles, then settled down for the night in the oak trees.

"I must get back before it's dark," said Usha to herself, as she hurried along the narrow path.

Already the sky was darkening. The clouds, black and threatening, loomed over Haunted Hill. This was the month for storms.

A deep rumble echoed over the hills, and Usha felt the first heavy drop of rain hit her cheek. She had

no umbrella with her; the weather had seemed so fine just a few hours ago. Now all she could do was tie an old scarf over her head, and pull her shawl tight across her shoulders. Holding the shopping bag close to her side, she quickened her pace. She was almost running. The raindrops came down faster now. Big heavy pellets of rain.

"I won't get home before the storm breaks," thought Usha. "I'll have to shelter in the ruins." She could only see a few feet ahead, but she knew the path well and she began to run.

Suddenly the wind sprang up again and brought the rain with a rush against her face. It was cold, stinging rain. She could hardly keep her eyes open. The wind hummed and whistled. It was behind her now, and helped her along, up the steep path and on to the brow of the hill.

There was another flash of lightning, followed by a peal of thunder. The ruins loomed up before her, grim and forbidding. But they would provide some shelter. It would be better than trying to go on. In the dark, in the howling wind, she had only to stray off the path to go over a rocky cliff-edge.

Who-whoo-whooo, howled the wind. She saw the wild plum tree swaying, bent double, its foliage thrashing against the ground. The broken walls did little to stop the wind.

Usha felt her way into the ruined building, helped by her memory and the constant flicker of lightning. She began moving along the wall, hoping to reach

the sheltered corner where a piece of the old roof remained. She placed her hands flat against the stones and moved sideways. Her hand touched something soft and furry. She gave a startled cry and snatched her hand away. Her cry was echoed by another cry – half snarl, half screech. Something leaped away in the dark.

It was only the wild cat that lived in the ruins. She had seen it often. She moved quickly along the wall until she heard the rain drumming on the remnant of the tin roof above her.

Once under it, crouching in the corner, she was sheltered from the wind and the rain. Above her, the tin sheets groaned and clattered, as if they would sail away at any moment. But they were held down by a solid branch from a straggling oak tree.

Usha remembered that across this empty room there was an old fireplace. There might be some shelter under the blocked up chimney. Perhaps it would be drier than it was in her corner. She decided not to attempt to find it just now. She might lose her way altogether.

Her clothes were soaked and the water streamed down from her long black hair. She stamped her feet to keep them warm. She thought she heard a faint cry. Was it the cat again, or an owl?

There had been no time to think of ghosts, but now she remembered her Grandfather's story about the lightning-blasted ruins. She hoped and prayed that lightning would not strike her as she sheltered there.

Thunder boomed over the hills, and the lightning came quicker now with only a few seconds between each flash.

Then there was a closer, brighter flash, and for a second the entire ruin was lit up. A blue streak sizzled across the floor: in at one end of the building, and out at the other.

It lit up the wall opposite and, Usha saw, crouching in the disused fireplace, two small figures. They could only be children! They looked up and stared back at her. And then everything was dark again.

Usha could hear her heart thudding. She had seen, without doubt, two ghosts at the other end of the room. She wasn't going to stay in the ruins a minute longer.

She ran out of her corner, toward the gap in the wall where she had entered. She was half-way across the open space when something – someone – fell against her. She stumbled, got up and again bumped into a soft and formless shape.

Usha screamed. There was another, echoing scream. And then there was a shout, a boy's voice, and she instantly recognized him.

"Suresh!" she shouted.

"Usha!"

"Binya!"

"It's me!"

"It's us!"

They tumbled into each other's arms, so surprised and relieved that all they could do was laugh and giggle and repeat each other's names.

Then Usha said, "I thought you were ghosts."

"We thought *you* were a ghost!" said Suresh.

"Come back under the roof," said Usha.

They huddled together in the corner, chattering excitedly.

"When it grew dark, we came looking for you," said Binya. "And then the storm broke."

"Shall we run back together?" asked Usha. "I don't want to stay here."

"We'll have to wait," said Binya. "The path's fallen away at one place. It won't be safe in the dark."

"We may have to wait till morning," wailed Suresh.

The wind and rain continued, and so did the thunder and lightning, but the children were not afraid now. They gave each other warmth and confidence. Even the ruins did not seem so forbidding.

After an hour the rain stopped and, although the wind still blew, it was now taking the clouds away and the thunder grew more distant. Then the wind, too, moved on. All was silent.

Towards dawn the whistling-thrush began to sing. Its sweet broken notes flooded the rain-washed ruins with music.

"We must go," said Usha.

"Come on," said Suresh, "I'm hungry."

As the sky grew lighter, they saw that the plum tree stood upright again, although it had lost all its blossoms. They stood outside the ruins, on the brow of the hill, watching the sky go from pink to red to orange. A light breeze sprang up.

When they were some distance from the ruins, Usha looked back and said, "Can you see something there, behind the wall? It looks like a hand waving to us."

"I can't see anything," said Suresh.

"It's just the top of the plum tree," said Binya.

They were on the path that went over the saddle
of the hill.

"Goodbye, goodbye . . ."

Voices on the wind.

"Who said goodbye?" asked Usha.

"Not I," said Suresh.

"Nor I," said Binya.

"I heard someone calling."

"It's only the wind."

Usha looked back. The sun had come up and was touching the tops of the ruined walls. The leaves of the plum tree shone brightly. The thrush sat there, singing.

"Come on," said Suresh. "I'm *hungry*."

"Goodbye, goodbye, goodbye ..."

Usha heard them calling. Or was it just the wind?

THE HAUNTING
(An excerpt)

Margaret Mahy

When, suddenly, on an ordinary Wednesday, it seemed to Barney that the world tilted and ran downhill in all directions, he knew he was about to be haunted again. It had happened when he was younger, but he had thought that being haunted was a babyish thing that you grew out of, like crying when you fell over, or not having a bike.

"Remember Barney's imaginary friends, Mantis, Bigbuzz, and Ghost?" Claire, his stepmother, sometimes said. "The garden seems empty now that they've gone. I quite miss them."

But she was really pleased, perhaps because, being so very real to Barney, they had become too real for her to laugh over. Barney had been sorry to lose them, but he wanted Claire to feel comfortable living with him. He could not remember his own mother and Claire had come as a wonderful surprise, giving him a hug when he came home from school, asking him about his day, telling him about hers, arranging picnics and unexpected parties and helping him with hard homework. It seemed worth losing Mantis, Bigbuzz, and Ghost and the other kind phantoms that had been his friends for so many days before Claire came.

Yet here it was beginning again . . . the faint dizzy twist in the world around him, the thin, singing drone as if some tiny insect were trapped in the curling mazes of his ear. Barney looked up at the sky, searching for a ghost, but there was only a great blueness like a weight pressing down on him. He looked away quickly, half expecting to be crushed into a sort of rolled-out gingerbread boy in an enormous stretched-out school uniform. Then he saw his ghost on the footpath beside him.

A figure was slowly forming out of the air: a child – quite a little one, only about four or five – struggling to be real. A curious, pale face grew clearer against a halo of shining hair, silver-gold hair that curled and crinkled, fading into the air like bright smoke. The child was smiling. It seemed to be having some difficulty in seeing Barney, so that he felt that *he* might be the one who was not quite real. Well, he was used to feeling that. In the days before Claire he had often felt that he himself couldn't be properly heard or seen. But then Mantis had taken time to become solid and Ghost had always been dim and smoky. So Barney was not too surprised to

see the ghost looking like a flat paper doll stuck against the air by some magician's glue. Then it became round and real, looking alive, but old-fashioned and strange, in its blue velvet suit and lace collar. A soft husky voice came out of it.

"Barnaby's dead!" it said. "Barnaby's dead! I'm going to be very lonely."

Barney stood absolutely still, feeling more tilted and dizzy than ever. His head rang as if it were strung like a bead on the thin humming that ran, like electricity, from ear to ear.

The ghost seemed to be announcing his death by his proper christened name of Barnaby – not just telling him he was going to die, but telling him that he was actually dead already. Now it spoke again.

"Barnaby's dead!" it said in exactly the same soft husky voice. "Barnaby's dead! I'm going to be very lonely." It wasn't just that it said the same words that it had said earlier. Its very tone – the lifts and flutterings of its voice – was exactly the same. If it had added, "This is a recorded message," it would not have seemed very out of place. Barney wanted to say something back to it, but what can you say to a ghost? You can't joke with it. Perhaps you could ask it questions, but Barney was afraid of the answers this ghost might give him. He would have to believe what it told him, and it might tell him something terrible.

As it turned out, this ghost was not one that would answer questions anyway. It had only one thing to say, and it had said it. It began to swing from side to side, like an absent-minded compass needle searching for some lost North. Its shape did not change but it swung widely and lay crossways in the air looking silly, but also very frightening.

"Barnaby's dead!" it said, "Barnaby's dead! And I'm going to be very lonely." Then it spun like a propeller, slowly at first, then faster and faster until it was only a blur of silver-gold in the air. It spun faster still until even the colours vanished and there

was nothing but a faint clear flicker. Then it stopped and the ordinary air closed over it. The humming in Barney's ears stopped, the world straightened out; time began again, the wind blew, trees moved, cars droned and tooted. Down through the air from the point where the ghost had disappeared fluttered a cloud of blue flakes. Barney caught a few of them in his hand. For a moment he held nothing but scraps of paper from a torn-up picture! He caught a glimpse of a blue velvet sleeve, a piece of lace cuff and a pink thumb and finger. Then the paper turned into quicksilver beads of colour that ran through his fingers and were lost before they fell on to the footpath.

Barney wanted to be at home at once. He did not want the in-between time of going down streets and around corners. There were no short cuts. He had to run all the way, fearing that at any moment he might be struck by lightning, or a truck, or by some terrible dissolving sickness that would eat him away as he ran. Little stumbles in his running made him think he might have been struck by bullets. His hair felt prickly and he wondered if it was turning white. He could imagine arriving at home and seeing his face in the hall mirror staring out under hair like cotton batting. He could imagine Claire saying, "Barney, what on earth have you been up to? Look at the state of your hair." How could he say, "Well, there was this ghost telling me that I was dead."

Claire would just say sternly, "Barney, have you been reading horror comics again?"

As it happened it was not Claire who met him when he got home but his two sisters, one on either side of the doorway: his thin, knobbly sister Troy, stormy in her black cloud of hair, her black eyebrows almost meeting over her long nose, and brown, round Tabitha, ready to talk and talk as she always did.

"Where have you been?" she asked. "You're late and have missed out on family news. But it's okay – the family novelist will now bring you up to date." By "the family novelist" Tabitha meant herself. She was writing the world's greatest novel, but no one was allowed to read it until she was twenty-one and it was published. However, she talked about it all the time and showed off by taking pages and pages of notes and talking about those, too.

"I stopped to . . ." Barney began. He felt his voice quaver and die out. He couldn't tell Tabitha about his ghost, particularly in front of Troy, who was five years older than he was and silent and scornful. But anyway Tabitha was not interested in his explanations. She was too busy telling him the family news in her own way.

"We are a house of mourning," she said in an important voice. "One of our dear relations has died. It's really good material for my novel and I'm taking notes like anything. No one I know has ever died before."

Barney stared in horror.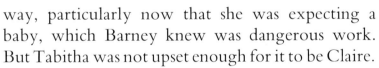

"Not Claire!" he began to say because he was always afraid that they would lose Claire in some way, particularly now that she was expecting a baby, which Barney knew was dangerous work. But Tabitha was not upset enough for it to be Claire.

"Great-Uncle Barnaby ... a scholar relation," she went on and then, as Barney's face stiffened and became blank she added, sarcastically, "You do remember him, don't you? You're named after him."

"I'm going to be very lonely," said a soft, husky voice in Barney's ear. He felt the world begin to slide away.

"Hey!" Troy's voice spoke on his other side. "You don't have to be upset. He was old ... and he'd been ill, very ill, for a while."

"It's not that!" Barney stammered. "I-I-I thought it might be me."

"Lonely!" said the echo in his haunted ear.

"I thought it *was* me," Barney said, and suddenly the world made up its mind and shrank away from him, grown to tennis ball size, then walnut size, then a pinhead of brightness in whirling darkness. On the steps of his own home Barney had fainted.

GHOST SOUP

*An Indian Tale
retold by John Paton*

A long time ago there lived a poor barber. The barber was poor because not enough people seemed to want their hair cut or their beards trimmed. This was the fashion at the time. The barber's wife was always complaining that she didn't have enough to eat. She would say to her husband, "If you did not have enough money to support a wife, why did you marry me? When I was in my father's house I had plenty to eat, but here there is never anything in the larder." Then she would take a broom and beat the poor barber until his back was quite blue.

One day, the barber was so stung by his wife's words – not to mention the broom – that he decided to leave the house and vowed never to return until he became rich. He packed a bag and set off, trudging the road from village to village, until he

143

came to the edge of a forest. His feet ached, so he lay down in the shade of a tall tree to bemoan his hard lot. "I must be the most unhappy barber in the land," he moaned, "perhaps in the whole world."

As the barber said this, something stirred in the branches of the tree above him. You see, this tree was the home of a ghost, and ghosts don't like people coming near their territory. As the ghost floated down, it spread its long white arms and stood like a tall palm tree before the barber, its gaping mouth hanging wide open. "Barber, you must suffer for disturbing me," cried the ghost. "I am going to destroy you, you miserable person."

The barber had never seen a ghost before, so he behaved as most people do when they first see one. His legs shook and the hair on his head stood straight up like the bristles on his wife's broom. But although he was frightened, the barber kept his head. "Oh, ghostly spirit," he said through chattering teeth, "I wonder whether you will destroy me when I show you what I have in my bag?"

"Stupid barber," replied the ghost, "how can the contents of your bag prevent me destroying you?" But he was an inquisitive ghost too, and he added, "Let me see what you have in your bag; then I will strike you dead."

The barber slowly opened his bag. "I hardly dare to say this to you, ghost, but my bag is full of ghosts I have captured during the last few days. In fact, there

is barely room for one more ghost in here before I
take them home for my good wife to make into
ghost soup. When I have captured you, ghost, and
squeezed you into my bag, I'll be on my way." So
saying, the barber took from his bag the mirror he
used to enable his customers to see whether their
beards had been trimmed to their taste. He stood up
and held the mirror right in front of the ghost's face.
"Here you see the last ghost I seized and bagged," he
said, "and now I am going to put you in my bag
with the others. My wife will be well pleased."

The ghost, seeing himself in the mirror, thought
it was another ghost. He was now convinced that
what the barber had said was true, and was filled
with fear. He did not at all relish the idea of being
part of the barber's wife's soup.

"Oh, sir barber," he whined, "I'll do whatever
you ask me to do, only don't put me in your bag. I'll
give you anything you want."

The barber now realized that the ghost was much
more frightened than he was, so he pulled himself up

to his full height and pointed a finger at the spirit before him. "I know you ghosts are a cunning crew," he said sternly, "How can I trust you? You will promise the earth and fail to keep your promise."

"Oh, sir," replied the ghost, "be merciful to me. I promise to bring you anything you ask for, no matter where on the earth it comes from, and if I don't bring it immediately you can put me in your bag with the other ghosts."

"Very well," said the barber, "bring me now a thousand gold pieces, and by tomorrow you must build a granary next to my house – a granary filled with wheat. Go now and fetch the gold pieces at once. If you fail to do as I ask you will most certainly be put into my bag."

At that, the ghost vanished, to reappear in less than a minute with a sack full of gold pieces. The barber peered into the sack and was overjoyed at the sight of so much wealth. At once he opened his bag and poured into it the thousand shining gold coins. Then, with a last warning to the ghost about the granary, the barber heaved the heavy bag onto his shoulder and set off for his home.

When the barber reached his house, it was the early hours of the morning. He beat proudly on the door and his wife climbed out of bed, grumbling at being disturbed at that hour. She unbolted the door and was amazed to see the barber pour a great heap of glittering coins onto the floor. At once, the woman felt sorry for the way in which she had treated the poor barber. She sat him down by the fire and made him as fine a meal as she could.

Next morning, the barber went outside to find a large granary standing solidly beside his little house – a granary full to overflowing with wheat.

Meanwhile, the ghost had floated back to his tree,

where he met his ghost uncle. He told his uncle what had happened, saying, "Whatever you do, avoid this terrible barber. If you meet him he will certainly put you in his bag, and you will end up in his wife's soup!"

"You fool!" said the ghost's uncle. "You think this barber can bag you! He is a cunning fellow and has cheated you."

"Oh no, uncle," wailed the ghost, "I saw with my own eyes a ghost the barber had bagged. If you do not believe me, go to the barber's house and you will see his power."

Muttering as to the stupidity of his nephew, the uncle ghost went off to the barber's house and peered in at the window.

The barber, sitting by the fire, knew that a ghost was around because of the cold blast of wind that whirled suddenly around the house and down the chimney. But the clever barber didn't move. He thought for a moment before saying to his wife, "My dear, I'd like nothing better for my supper than a bowl of your delicious ghost soup."

At this, the ghostly face at the window began to look decidedly uneasy. The barber caught a glimpse of this face out of the corner of his eye as he got out of his chair, went to his bag and took out his mirror. Holding the mirror behind him, the barber approached the window, then, all of a sudden, he held it up right in front of the ghost's face on the other side of the glass. There was a piercing screech as the uncle ghost vanished at the speed of light.

Next morning, when the barber went outside, he found another large granary on the other side of his house. It was full to bursting with fine rice, and on the floor were two thousand gold coins glittering in the morning sun.

So the barber became a rich man, and he lived for many happy years with a wife who never beat him. And one thing is certain; they were never at any time haunted by silly ghosts.

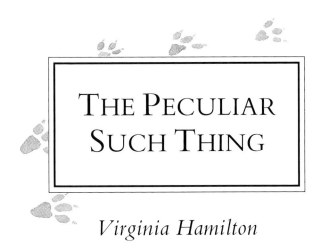

THE PECULIAR
SUCH THING

Virginia Hamilton

A long time ago way off in the high piney woods lived a fellow all alone. He lived in a one-room log cabin. There was a big old fireplace, and that is where this fellow cooked his supper to eat it right in front of the fire.

One night, after the fellow had cooked and ate his supper, somethin crept through the cracks of the cabin logs. That somethin was the most peculiar such thing the fellow ever saw. And it had a *great, big, long tail.*

As soon as the fellow saw that somethin with its *great, big, long tail,* he reached for his axe. With a swoopin strike with it, he cut the somethin's tail clean off. The peculiar such thing crept away through the cracks between the logs, and was gone.

This fellow, like he had no sense, he cooked the *great, big, long tail.* Yes, he did. It tasted sweet and he ate it. Goodness! And then he went to bed, and in a little while he went off to sleep.

The fellow hadn't been asleep very long before he woke right up again. He heard somethin climbin up the side of his cabin. It sounded mighty like a cat. He could hear it scratchin and tearin away. And pretty soon he heard it say, *"Tailypo, tailypo. Give me back my tailypo."*

Now the fellow livin there all alone did have some dogs. Big one was Best and the other two slight ones was All Right and Fair. And when that fellow heard somethin, he called his dogs, "Yuh! Dawgs! Come on!" like that. And his dogs come flyin out from under the cabin. And they chased the peculiar such thing away down a far piece. Then this fellow went on back to bed. He went to sleep.

It was deep in the middle of the next night when the fellow woke up. He heard somethin by his front door tryin to get in. He listened hard and he could

hear it scratchin and tearin away. And he heard it say, *"Tailypo, tailypo. Give me back my tailypo."*

Fellow sat up in his bed. He called his dogs, "Yuh! You, Best, you All Right, you Fair, come on in!" like that. And the dogs busted around the corner. And they caught up with the peculiar such thing at the gate, and they broke they own tails tryin to catch it. This time they chased what it was down into the big hollow there. And the fellow, well, he went back to bed and went to sleep.

It was way long toward mornin, the fellow woke up and he hears somethin down in the big swamp. He had to listen. He heard it say, *"You know you got it. I know you know. Give me back my tailypo."*

That man sat up in bed. He called his dogs, "You the Best, you All Right, and you Fair. Yuh! Come on in here!"

Well, this time, the dogs never come. The thing down there in the hollow musta carried them off in there. It musta eaten the first one, says, *"That's best."* It eaten the other two, says *"That ain't but all right and fair."*

And the fellow went back to bed. Don't see how he could sleep again. But he didn't know how bad off his dogs was by then.

Well, it was just daybreak. The fellow was awake. Scared, he didn't know why. Musta heard somethin. Somethin right there with him in the room. It sounded like a cat climbin up the covers at the foot of his bed. He listened. He could hear it, scratchin and tearin away.

The fellow look at the foot of his bed. He's seein two little pointy ears comin up over the edge of the bed. In another minute, he's seein two big, scary-red eyeballs lookin straight at him. He can't say nothin. He can't scream, he's too scared to death.

That peculiar such thing at the foot of the bed kept on creepin up, creepin up. By and by, it was right on top of the fellow. And it said in his face in a real low voice, *"Tailypo, tailypo. Give me back my tailypo."*

That man loses his voice, loses his power of

speech. But finally, he can say it. Says, "I hasn't got it. I hasn't got your tailypo!"

And that somethin that was there, that peculiar such thing, says right back, *"Yes you has!"* It jumped on that fellow and it was fierce. Its big teeth tore at him, made him ribbons. They say it got its tailypo back.

Fellow's cabin fall to ruin. It rot. It crumble and it disappear. Nothin left to it in the big woods but the place where it was.

And the folks that live near that place say that deep in the night, when the moon is goin down and the wind blows across the place just right, you can hear some peculiar such thing callin, *"Tailypo, tailypo ..."* like that. And then, the sound of it do just fade away with the moonlight. Like it never even ever was.

THE HAIRY TOE

Anonymous

Once there was a woman went out to pick beans,
and she found a Hairy Toe.
She took the Hairy Toe home with her,
and that night, when she went to bed,
the wind began to moan and groan.
Away off in the distance
she seemed to hear a voice crying,
"Where's my Hair-r-ry To-o-oe?
Who's got my Hair-r-ry To-o-oe?"

The woman crept down,
way down under the covers,
and about that time
the wind appeared to hit the house,

smoosh,

and the old house creaked and cracked

like something was trying to get in.
The voice had come nearer,
almost at the door now,
and it said,
"Where's my Hair-r-ry To-o-oe?
Who's got my Hair-r-ry To-o-oe?"

The woman crept further down
under the covers
and pulled them tight around her head.

The wind growled around the house
like some big animal
and r-r-um-mbled
over the chimbley.
All at once she heard the door cr-r-a-ack
and Something slipped in
and began to creep over the floor.

The floor went
cr-e-eak, cre-e-ak
at every step that thing took towards her bed.
The woman could almost feel
it bending over her bed.
Then in an awful voice it said:
"Where's my Hair-r-ry To-o-oe?
Who's got my Hair-r-ry To-o-oe?
You've got it!"

For permission to reproduce copyright material acknowledgement and thanks are due to the following:

Methuen Children's Books for "The Guitarist" from *Mouth Open Story Jump Out* by Grace Hallworth. Prentice Hall/A Division of Simon & Schuster for "In a Dark, Dark Box" by Jane Hollowood from *Spooky* edited by Pamela Lonsdale. Susan Price for "The Fraid", copyright © Susan Price 1992. McIntosh and Otis, Inc. for "The House that Lacked a Bogle" by Sorche Nic Leodhas from *Gaelic Ghosts* published by Holt, Reinhart, & Winston Inc. Sydney J. Bounds for "The Ghost Train", copyright © Sydney J. Bounds 1972. Philomel Books for "A Story About Death" from *A Taste for Quiet* by Judith Gorog © 1982. Blackie and Son Ltd. for "Shiver and Shake" from *Grimm's Fairy Tales* retold by Amabel Williams-Ellis, copyright © 1959 Blackie and Son Ltd. and Amabel Williams-Ellis. Murray Pollinger for "They Wait" from *They Wait and Other Spine Chillers* by Jan Mark. Ruskin Bond for "The Wind on Haunted Hill". J. M. Dent & Sons Ltd for the excerpt from *The Haunting* by Margaret Mahy, copyright © 1982 Margaret Mahy. Alfred A. Knopf, Inc. for "The Peculiar Such Thing" from *The People Could Fly: American Black Folktales*, told by Virginia Hamilton, copyright © 1985 Virginia Hamilton. "Ghost Soup" retold by John Paton (1992) copyright © Grisewood & Dempsey Ltd.

Every effort has been made to obtain permission from copyright holders. If, regrettably, any omissions have been made, we shall be pleased to make suitable corrections in any reprint.